MW00628955

TERROR ON THE TRACKS!

I felt the train behind me like a huge angry iron beast. Then I saw the station ramp and a smocked workman staring into the tunnel.

Like a runner reaching the finish, I threw out my arms and staggered the rest of the way. Behind me there was a sudden bang and a blue flash. He'd shot at me at last—but he'd missed!

There was a loud squeal of brakes, and the train ground to a shuddering halt on the tracks. I no longer cared. "Save me!" I sobbed, and fell into the workman's arms.

MYSTERY OF
THE METRO

BY ELIZABETH HOWARD

ILLUSTRATED BY

MICHAEL WM. KALUTA

A BYRON PREISS BOOK

RANDOM HOUSE 🏠 NEW YORK

Copyright © 1987 by Byron Preiss Visual Publications, Inc. All rights reserved under International and Pan-American Copyright Conventions. Published in the United States by Random House, Inc., New York, and simultaneously in Canada by Random House of Canada Limited, Toronto.

Library of Congress Cataloging-in-Publication Data:
Howard, Elizabeth. Mystery of the metro.
  (My name is Paris) "A Byron Preiss book."
  SUMMARY: In 1900, sixteen-year-old Paris, a Chicago teenager with a fondness for Sherlock Holmes, travels to Paris, France, to visit her uncle, a prominent scientist, only to find on her arrival that he has died under circumstances sufficiently mysterious to make her determined to investigate on her own. [1. Mystery and detective stories. 2. Paris (France)—Fiction] I. Kaluta, Michael William, ill. II. Title. III. Series: Howard, Elizabeth. My name is Paris. PZ7.H8327My 1987 [Fic] 86-21964 ISBN: 0-394-87546-X (trade); 0-394-97546-4 (lib. bdg.)

Manufactured in the United States of America   1   2   3   4   5   6   7   8   9   0

Special thanks to Michael Hardwick, Mollie Hardwick, Stephanie Spinner, Janet Schulman, Ellen Steiber, Tisha Hamilton, and Joan Brandt.

Book design by Alex Jay
Cover design by Alex Jay
Cover painting by Michael Wm. Kaluta
Edited by Ruth Ashby

MY NAME IS PARIS is a trademark of Byron Preiss Visual Publications, Inc.

MY NAME IS

PARIS

CHAPTER 1

When I look back and try to see how I got into trouble as quickly as I did, I must admit that my loose tongue was to blame. I suppose I have always been somewhat outspoken, but I have taken this to be an advantage, the reflection of a strong, honest character. There are others, as you will see, who are not of the same opinion.

The first warning that I was headed for trouble came two years ago when I was still in Chicago. Mrs. Grundy, my homemaking teacher, had just informed me in no uncertain terms that I had very little chance of turning into a lady. Before I knew it, I had replied that I had no interest in becoming a

lady; I would gladly settle for being a woman. Now, if I'd only left it at that, things wouldn't have been so bad. But I finished by saying that Mrs. Grundy might try being less of a lady and more of a woman herself.

That clever comment nearly got me expelled from school. Worse, when Papa found out, he was absolutely furious. First thing the next morning, he escorted me to school and made me apologize for my appalling behavior and wretched manners. I did my best to sound remorseful, but it was not easy, particularly since Papa was making apologies too.

"Paris MacKenzie, you should have known better," my mother said that night. "Your father is a Frenchman—he expects you to treat others with the same respect that he does. When you insulted your teacher, you dishonored him."

Now I understand what my mother meant, but at the time I thought everyone was making a great fuss over nothing. Here in Paris what my father calls an overhasty tongue is even less appreciated than it is back home. In fact, in France many things are done differently than they are in Chicago. Yet I'm getting ahead of myself. My adventure, as I call it, started on what should have been the most wonderful day of my life.

It was April 30, 1900, and I was on my way by sea to spend a year in France. According to my parents, I was going in order to "broaden my cultural horizons." As Papa put it, "We hope you will

learn a great deal from an exposure to fine art and architecture." It was also hoped that my French would improve. My reasons for wanting to live in France were far simpler. I wanted to spend my days sitting at sidewalk cafés and my evenings becoming a chic woman of the world. I fantasized that I'd become so sophisticated that my style would be worthy of my name at last!

Of course I was already the envy of everyone back home when I announced I was going. "Think of the Frenchmen!" my best friend Edith whispered to me. "I'm sure they're all tall, dark, and handsome, with carnations in their buttonholes and tall silk top hats. All *très distingué* . . . very distinguished."

"Mais bien sûr, ma chérie," I answered. "But of course, my dear." I'd been trying madly to brush up on my French, but I still couldn't believe I was really going to have to use it!

The trip had all come about so unexpectedly. It was right after last Christmas, and Brannigan, our Irish butler, came looking for me in my room, to say that my parents wanted to see me in Papa's study. I was lost in *The Memoirs of Sherlock Holmes,* my Christmas present from Papa, and I had been putting myself in the place of the famous detective, tracking a particularly notorious criminal through the murky streets of London, when Brannigan's knock on the door made me jump.

I straightened my dress and hair and went on down.

"Darling," Mama greeted me. "Papa and I have an extra Christmas present for you."

"But I already have the dressing-table set and Sherlock Holmes," I said.

"This is something else. Something very special."

I must have looked perplexed, for Papa didn't keep me guessing any longer.

"Uncle Claude has invited you over to stay."

"In—in—France? *Paris!* Mama! It's—"

They laughed at my amazement. I don't think I'd ever been so thrilled before. Or so tongue-tied.

"It's wonderful!" I gasped at last. "How soon do we go? In the new year?"

I'd never met my French uncle Claude, Papa's only brother, but he wrote regularly, and I knew that he and Papa were very close. He was a doctor in Paris who specialized in chemical research.

"The invitation is for you alone," said Papa. "Mama and I have to go on with our work."

Actually, although I was merely surprised, I must have looked a little taken aback. Mama said quickly, "But you're to remember, dear, that you're free to come back whenever you wish. Any reason at all, and you need only say the word to Uncle."

"We'll miss you enormously," Papa added. "But Uncle Claude seems to think that a year in Europe would be very educational for you, and we agree. I must also admit a certain yearning for you to fully experience my native country, but you must decide for yourself."

It didn't take much deciding! By that evening my plans were set, and the next few months were filled with the bustle of shopping and other preparations.

Mama was quite concerned that I have a female companion on the ocean voyage. She wasn't worried for propriety's sake, since she has always been an advocate of women's independence. But as a physician, she had heard many tales, and she was sure I would find myself absolutely "at sea" without someone I already knew. She was quite relieved, then, to find that Muriel Hooper was traveling to France at the same time.

Mama had met Muriel through one of her many charities, the Ladies' Society for the Care and Feeding of the Homeless.

"Muriel is a good and kind woman," Mama told me, "but she has her eccentricities. I trust you will be most polite to her, even when you disagree." Mama gave me a meaningful look.

I now wonder if Mama knew just how eccentric Muriel Hooper really was. She was traveling to Paris to attend the Third Annual Conference for Research into the Realm of the Paranormal. *Paranormal* was the key word for Muriel. Anything that was just plain normal bored her. Tarot cards, séances, crystal balls, ghosts, mental telepathy—the weirder it was, the more it seemed to fascinate her. She had been trying to read my

palm ever since the trip had begun, but I'd steadfastly refused. Mama had always told me that such things were superstitious nonsense.

Fortunately, despite her eccentricities, Muriel was one of the warmest, most interesting people I'd ever met. We spent the long days on the ocean voyage discussing her passion, the occult, and mine—Sherlock Holmes.

Like most everyone else, I was a Sherlock Holmes addict. At school we would call one another "My dear Watson" and keep exclaiming "Elementary!" whenever we could. We had all gotten past considering Holmes's exploits made-up stories. He and Dr. Watson, and their lodgings in Baker Street, were more real to us than many things we could see and touch.

I have to admit I was surprised to find that Muriel had read as much of Sherlock Holmes as I had. Of course, her reasons were different. She assured me that Holmes's creator, Arthur Conan Doyle, was extremely interested in the supernatural and had been known to attend séances in London.

I found it hard to believe that anyone with such a clear mind would indulge in such hogwash. "I'll believe it when I see Holmes attend a séance," I told her.

Muriel just gave me one of her patient smiles and said, "There are more things in heaven and on earth than are dreamt of in your philosophy class, Paris. Someday, when you least expect it, you will find that out."

Now the steamship that had brought us from New York was heading toward the coast of France. In vain, I peered through the fog and tried to catch the first glimpse of the new country before me.

Then, like a stage curtain rising on a scene, the mist was lifted by a sudden breeze and I could see France for the first time.

"Look!" I gasped. "White cliffs!"

Muriel looked eagerly over the railing with me. We saw an undulating line of grass-topped, chalk cliffs, spotted by an occasional house or barn.

Suddenly the sun came bursting through the clouds and the land turned a brilliant emerald green.

"You see, Paris," Muriel said. "The sun has come out! This is a sign that your stay in France will be a happy one!"

I turned and grinned. Muriel was forever finding omens in things, from the way the tea leaves settled in my cup to the kinds of birds that flew overhead during our voyage.

"Muriel," I said, determined to ignore this talk of signs, "I'm going to enjoy France with or without the sun's approval!"

Soon we could see the white stone docks of Le Havre itself. On the Quai des Transatlantiques a crowd of people waited, shouting and waving black top hats and derbies and handkerchiefs. Men in blue smocks and black caps with shiny peaks lined the wharves. The

sky was crisscrossed by the masts of dozens of small fishing boats, whalers, and transatlantic steamers.

I felt overwhelmed by the newness of it all. All at once I wanted to know what would happen when I stepped off the boat onto that foreign shore. Impulsively I grabbed Muriel by the hand.

"Muriel," I said, "tell my fortune! Tell me what Europe will be like!"

Muriel laughed. "I knew your curiosity would overcome you at last." She took my right hand and spread my palm outward over her own. For a moment, in the midst of all that noise and confusion, we were silent.

Then she spoke. "Your palm is in perfect proportion to your fingers, indicating a well-balanced mind, impressionable and intelligent. I discern a tendency toward impulsive action, which you can only control by judgment that you often abandon. The prominence of your Mount of Mercury indicates spirit, independence, and a penchant for travel and adventure."

I knew nothing about my Mount of Mercury, but I smiled and she continued with utmost sincerity.

"Your line of life, I'm happy to say, extends well around the ball of your thumb. It is broken up at numerous points, however, where your life might be threatened. . . ." Muriel looked at me thoughtfully. "You are just past sixteen, aren't you? I'd say one of these threats is very close at hand."

"Are you trying to scare me?" I asked. When Muriel didn't answer, I decided to let the matter go. I didn't believe in this stuff anyway. "Well, what about men?" I said. "Am I going to fall in love?"

"These little lines here indicate that you will experience one, perhaps two, serious affairs of the heart in the near future." Muriel sounded a bit abstracted, as if her mind were elsewhere.

"Anything else?" I guess some of my skepticism showed through, for Muriel looked at my hand once again as if it were the very mirror of fate itself.

"There is one more thing." Muriel spoke very slowly. "In the science of palmistry, there is one sure sign of danger, perhaps the most important thing to look for in a hand. You have two stars, one here and one here." She pointed out two little circles of intersecting lines. "The one signifies a great fatality, possibly even murder. The other indicates a misfortune—brought about not by a man, but by a woman."

As she spoke the ship gave one last vibration, and then came to a dead halt. I had landed in France, but the exhilaration was gone. In its place was a sense of foreboding—that this trip would be far different from what Uncle Claude and my parents had had in mind!

CHAPTER 2

"I am sorry, Paris, but those of us who take the science of palmistry seriously cannot hide what we see," Muriel said softly. "You have no need to be frightened. Like every science, palmistry is flawed. My reading is only an interpretation."

Feeling only slightly reassured by her words, I removed my uncle's photograph from my purse and scanned the crowd for him. The photograph showed a balding man with a round face and a dark, perfectly trimmed mustache. His eyes were like my father's—shrewd and watchful but with deep creases at their outer edges. They were the eyes of a man who had spent a lot of time laughing.

"Do you see him?" Muriel asked.

I searched the crowd again, but in all that sea of upturned faces and waving hands there wasn't anyone who resembled my uncle.

"No, not yet."

"Well, I hope he shows up soon." Muriel sounded unusually troubled. "The opening lecture of the conference is scheduled to begin this afternoon at one thirty and I'd hate to miss any part of it."

"I'm sure he'll be here any moment," I reassured her, feeling more concerned for her than for myself.

"Perhaps your uncle left a message," Muriel suggested. "There must be a bureau."

One of the officials on the wharf escorted us to the inquiry office. There, the clerk frowned sympathetically as he said that he knew of no message for me.

"I guess I'll just have to wait," I said.

"What time does the next train leave for Paris?" Muriel asked the young man.

"At half past noon, madame," he replied in studied English. "Your ship arrived a little late due to the fog. You should go straight to the station, as there will not be another train until ten minutes past three."

Both Muriel and I knew that it took almost an hour to reach Paris by train. If she didn't leave now, she would miss the lecture.

"You go ahead," I told her. "I'll be perfectly fine."

"Your mother would—"

"My mother will never know," I promised. "You came so far for this conference. You can't miss this train."

Muriel still looked worried, but I could see her weakening. "Are you sure?" she asked. I nodded. Then she kissed me good-bye, tendered apologies for her "hobby," and hurried off.

As I watched her leave, I suddenly realized that of all the hundreds of passengers on the ship I was the only one still on the wharf.

"I will take your baggage, mademoiselle." Behind me, the shipping-line man had picked up my bag. I followed him as he carried it to the ladies' waiting lounge, a huge, musty room that looked as though no one had thought to wait there in centuries.

"And I don't blame them," I thought as I tried to get comfortable on one of the hard wooden benches. For a while I tried reading my new Sherlock Holmes, but it was no use. I would read half a page and then my mind would wander back to Muriel's prediction that "one of these threats is very close at hand."

After a while I got up and started pacing. "Buck up, Paris MacKenzie," I told myself sternly. "Uncle will be here soon. There's no use in falling to pieces. He's not going to want a hysterical niece on his hands." Still, I had to consider what I would do if he didn't appear.

Abruptly, I stopped pacing. This was getting ridiculous. A MacKenzie did not let herself get

thrown by a change in plans. For whatever reason, my uncle had not made it to the station. That meant it was up to me to find *him*.

The 3:10 train to Paris was due to leave in half an hour. I gathered my possessions together and marched back to the bureau, where I left a note for Uncle Claude, just in case he should come. Then I found my way to the train terminal, bought a first-class ticket, and boarded the train.

As I looked out the window, France sped past, mile upon mile of flat, green countryside. Farmers were bent double over their crops, their thatched cottages dotting the landscape. Cows and sheep grazed contentedly in the pastures, and in one field a dozen young horses raced as if they could never get enough of running. Despite my worries, I was quickly charmed. It was as if I were seeing the world with new eyes.

Not until the train arrived at the Gare St.-Lazare did I realize just how foreign everything would be. Up until then, everyone I'd encountered had spoken English, and it didn't even occur to me to worry about language problems. After all, back in Chicago, I'd done reasonably well in French class, and had even practiced some with Papa before coming over. Now, after waiting in line for what felt like hours, I could only stare blankly at the customs officials as they fired questions at me. I understood about every third word. Determined not to get flustered, I patiently asked them to repeat just about everything they said. And then, when I had a rough idea of what the given question was, I discovered just how long it could take a person to come up with a one-sentence reply. I think I must have been boring everyone to death, because finally one official gave me a weary look and waved me through.

The next step was easier. I held out a few francs to a man who looked like a porter, and he trundled my baggage outside the station and hailed a cab for me. The cab was every bit as grimy as the ones back home, but I wasn't about to attempt to complain.

"*Numéro vingt-six, rue Cambon,*" I said in my most careful French. The driver heaved my bags on top of the carriage without even glancing at me, then climbed back up and took the reins.

Dusk was just beginning to fall, and the streets were crowded with vehicles of all sorts, motor and horse-drawn. For the first time I noticed the distinctive smell of Paris, a mixture of tobacco, horses, cooking, and musty perfume. It was wonderful.

The peculiar vividness of sight that I had experienced on the train came back again, and the world outside the cab took on an unearthly bright clarity. The colored lights strung out over the city tinted the fountains and trees and buildings red, yellow, and green. I remembered what I had momentarily forgotten—that the Grand Exposition had just opened this month!

I'd read about the exposition back home in

Chicago. It had attracted thousands of exhibits from all over the world, and a veritable second city had been built along the banks of the river Seine in order to accommodate them. From the cab I could see a whole hodgepodge of shapes outlined against the sky: domes, minarets, steeples, and towers. The Eiffel Tower soared above the whole scene, reaching hundreds of feet skyward. Even as I looked at it, the thousands of electric bulbs outlining the entire metal structure blinked into glowing life. "If only Mama and Papa were here to see it!" I thought.

The cab ride went on and on, and my excitement dimmed. Where was I being taken?

"Stop worrying," I told myself briskly. But for some reason Muriel's words about a great fatality in my future came back to me. What if the fatality were mine!

I looked out the window at the deserted streets. If I screamed, I'd never be heard . . .

Suddenly the driver called out *"Numéro vingt-six, mam'selle."* And the cab stopped, along with my troubling thoughts.

There it was, number 26, rue Cambon, with light shining through the open front door.

But why was there a crowd outside? And that uniformed figure standing stiffly beside the door—surely that was a policeman!

In a moment I was out of the cab and in the crowd.

"Qu'est-ce que—" I began, and promptly for-

got the rest of the phrase for "What has happened?"

Though no one bothered to answer, I was certain something was wrong. "Please. *S'il vous plaît*," I went on desperately. "Let me through!"

"Mademoiselle!" The cabby was standing behind me, holding my baggage and looking quite annoyed. I realized I'd neglected to pay him. As I counted out the fare I managed to calm down enough to remember the phrase for "What is going on?" He turned and spoke rapidly to the man in front of me.

"C'est meurtre!" was the reply.

Although it was a word I'd never had to learn, it was so like its English equivalent, and was said in such a tone, that there was no mistaking its meaning: *murder!*

Now I made no attempt to be polite, but simply pushed my way through the crowd. As I reached the door, the gendarme's attention was distracted by the flare of a photographer's flash powder. I darted past him.

And halted abruptly. Several men stood silent around the doorway of a room at the end of the hall. Their attention was on something within, I saw as I drew closer; it was a body under a white sheet. Someone pulled the sheet back and the face was exposed. It was contorted in pain, ashen, absolutely still.

"Uncle Claude!" I cried. Before I could say anything else, I felt the floor vanish beneath me.

I was lying on a couch in a big, high-ceilinged room. I turned my head and glimpsed tapestries, fine upholstery and carpeting, the glitter of glass and porcelain.

A middle-aged man in a dark suit was bending over me. He had a small white beard and an anxious look on his face.

He held a glass out to me. There was some brown liquid in it which had a medicinal smell that I didn't care for. All the same, I took a sip and immediately felt my lips and tongue burn. I gagged a little and realized that it was brandy.

I am not the fainting type, but, like it or not, I had passed out.

It was then that I remembered

the body—my uncle Claude's body—lying
sprawled on the carpet. I saw those twisted features again and closed my eyes, but that only
made the recollection clearer.

"Take another little drink, my dear," the man
with the beard said in accented but good English, and I obeyed. This time I felt better for it.

I moved to sit up a little, and the man helped
me gently. He wore a serious expression, but his
eyes showed relief.

A woman in a black, high-collared dress stood
behind him. Though her face was plain, there
was something reassuring about it. Her beauty
was in her hair; it was thick and silver, and she
wore it swept up into one of those perfect knots
I've never been able to master. She was obviously the housekeeper, because a ring of keys
hung from a chain that encircled her waist. She
stood erect, with her hands clasped before her.
Even in my confused state I could sum her up in
a word: competence.

Standing beside the open French doors was
another man. Young and burly, he showed no
emotion, but stared at me as if I were a remotely
interesting scientific specimen.

I swallowed hard, wondering what I should
say. At least I didn't need to ask where I was. It
was clear that I was in Uncle's sitting room.

The man with the beard spoke first. "Do you
find yourself better, Mademoiselle Paris?" he in-
quired.

That was a surprise.

"How—how do you know my name?"

"It is on your baggage, of course. And you were expected. It grieves me to make your acquaintance under such tragic circumstances. I am Dr. Levine. I have—*had*—the honor to be your uncle's close friend."

"How do you do, Doctor?" I answered with what I hoped was a polite smile.

The doctor turned to the woman and the other man. "Permit me to introduce Detective Latour of the Criminal Investigation Department," he said. "Also, Madame Frenais. Madame is the late Dr. MacKenzie's housekeeper."

Madame Frenais made an effort to smile, though she was clearly very upset.

The detective spoke for the first time, also in English, although not as good as the doctor's.

"You are Mademoiselle Paris MacKenzie, of Chicago?"

"I thought you knew that," I said. Detective Latour was only doing his job, but something about the man made me impatient.

"It is necessary to establish it formally, mademoiselle."

"All right. I am."

"Parlez-vous français, mademoiselle?" he asked so abruptly that it sounded like he was trying to catch me off-guard. I decided I didn't *parle français* for the time being. Let him struggle on in my language.

"Not too well," I answered truthfully. "I'm here to learn."

There was a question *I* needed to ask. "Someone in the crowd out front . . . someone mentioned murder. My uncle . . . ?"

I'd turned to Dr. Levine, but he stood silently, refusing to meet my eyes.

It was Detective Latour who replied. "No, no! Rumors. That is how they start. The crowd has been sent away now."

"Well, then how—"

Dr. Levine broke in. "I am desolate, my dear young lady, to have to say that your uncle suffered a heart attack earlier today. It will console you to know that he died quickly, without pain."

Those contorted features sprang back vividly to my mind. I'd never seen such a look of pain!

"Had he been taken ill?" I asked. "Were you with him, Doctor?"

"No. Not *with* him."

"Madame Frenais?" I asked.

"I was—" she began, but before she could finish Latour interrupted.

"The facts are as follows. Late this morning the maid entered the study to air it out. She found Dr. MacKenzie there, where he had fallen.

"There had been a burglary," Latour went on dispassionately. "A break-in. It is obvious that your uncle disturbed the intruder. They grappled with each other and the exertion proved too much for the doctor's heart."

I'd gotten into the habit of observing and thinking things out as Sherlock Holmes might. The object was to spot things that other people either missed or took for granted. Papa said it was a good habit, and encouraged me. Now I glanced briefly around this richly appointed sitting room. Pictures, vases, and other objects obviously belonging to Uncle's fine Art Nouveau collection were everywhere. There was no sign of a burglary.

"What was stolen?" I asked.

"Nothing has been found missing," answered Latour.

"Then how can you be sure . . . ?"

"The study is in disarray. A window was found wide open. My conclusion as to what occurred is quite definite, mademoiselle, and I shall report accordingly to the coroner."

"Pompous as well as rude," I thought.

Dr. Levine tried to explain more kindly. "The intruder would not risk lingering, on finding that he had been the cause of a death. He would make his escape immediately, taking nothing which would connect him with this house—in case he should be stopped by the police."

"This happened last night, then?" I asked.

"It was sometime this morning," Dr. Levine replied. "Your uncle's bed had been slept in. Since he was fully dressed when the maid found him, it is obvious that he had been preparing to set off for Le Havre to meet you. He must have looked into his study briefly, and unfortunately . . . "

This sounded so odd that I just had to say, "I never heard of anyone being burgled just when all the household's ready to wake up!"

"It is only in storybooks that thieves confine themselves to the dead of night," Latour said stiffly. "Mademoiselle will discover, when she is older, that real life is not the same as fiction."

I have never liked being addressed as if I were an imbecile.

"It might do you some good to read a storybook," I told him. "There are a lot of policemen who admit they've learned from Sherlock Holmes."

"*American* policemen, no doubt?" Latour said, smiling for the first time.

"English, too," I retorted. I'd read that somewhere.

"So, Monsieur Sherlock Holmes and the English police would have reached a different conclusion about this business, eh? The Frenchman on the spot counts for nothing, you are saying?"

"I'm not saying that at all, Monsieur Latour."

"Perhaps Mademoiselle will tell us what her English hero would have made of the evidence here?"

"Of course I can't," I snapped back. "Dr. Levine said my uncle was all ready to go and meet me at the ship. So the servants must have been awake to get him his breakfast and drive him to the station. The lights would have been on too." I stopped myself, realizing that shock was giving way to curiosity—curiosity and a strong determination to find out what had really happened to my uncle.

"Since you ask me what Sherlock Holmes

would have thought," I went on, "I guess it's that no burglar in the world would have risked breaking in then. I apologize for seeming rude, Monsieur Latour. But it's *my* uncle who died—or got killed—so it's reasonable to ask questions, isn't it?"

I wasn't sure whether what I saw in his eyes was astonishment at the new experience of being interrogated by a girl or chagrin because I had hit on something he had overlooked.

The chief effect it had, however, was to make those stern features of his relax. He actually grinned and said, "Bravo!"

That quite took me aback. Just as unexpected was the sound of Mme. Frenais's voice addressing me. Her English was careful and painstakingly correct.

"There is no mystery, mademoiselle. The late doctor was always most considerate to all his servants. He told me yesterday evening that he would not require us to disturb ourselves. He would let himself out early and take a cab to the station. He intended to breakfast on the train."

So much for that. I knew without looking at him that Detective Latour was watching me. Either he wanted to see me confounded, or he was curious about anything else I might come up with. I gave up for the moment.

"The body will have been removed by now," Latour said briskly. "Now, if you will excuse me, I have some final things to attend to."

As he left the room he beckoned to Mme.

Frenais to follow. The door closed behind them, and Dr. Levine reached down to take my pulse.

"Poor child!" he said. "To arrive to such a tragedy! It is quite dreadful. I myself am quite desolated—but you . . ."

He seemed satisfied with my pulse, but he held my hand comfortingly.

"I scarcely knew Uncle Claude, Doctor," I said. "As his close friend, it's *you* who should have *my* sympathy."

"That is a most gracious thought, my dear," he replied, and bent his head. For the first time I had the delicious experience of a man's lips brushing the back of my hand.

But my curiosity still needed satisfying.

"Doctor . . ."

"Yes, my dear?"

"Am I being told the truth . . . about how it happened?"

He hesitated before answering. "It is the police who form theories, not I. Latour is a senior detective. It is because he was away from Paris this morning that the . . . that your uncle had to be left where he was found for so long. They wanted Latour to investigate everything personally. He arrived not very long before you."

"So you didn't examine Uncle yourself?"

"I was requested not to touch him. However, the police surgeon is well known to me. He assured me that it had been a heart attack. Truly, you may believe that."

Even so, Uncle's poor, twisted face haunted me.

"And there really *had* been a burglary?"

"I saw the open window myself. There were drawers pulled out and papers strewn everywhere. What other explanation could there be?"

What, indeed?

I had brashly cross-questioned the investigating detective. He had not put me in my place, but rather had let me do that to myself.

The housekeeper had quite plausible answers to my clever observations about the domestic routine.

Uncle's "close friend," Dr. Levine, could add nothing more for me.

Couldn't—or *wouldn't?* I recalled his unwillingness to meet my eyes earlier.

Maybe he was being kind. Maybe he knew more, but wanted to spare me from it. But Latour was a different matter. Could he, with his fine reputation, be as rigid and singleminded as Inspector Lestrade and the other Scotland Yarders that Sherlock Holmes was so scornful of?

My sense of perspective suddenly returned. The aftermath of real-life tragedy wasn't the time for clever games. The sensible thing would be to accept what the detective and the housekeeper had said, and what Dr. Levine seemed to want me to believe.

The trouble was, I couldn't.

CHAPTER
4

Dr. Levine was speaking again. "Paris, my dear—if I may address you so?—how are you feeling now?"

"Much better, thank you."

He peered at me closely. "Yes, your color is returning. Paris, I must apologize for your not being met at Le Havre. I tried to send a servant to the wharf office with word that you were to take the first train leaving after the boat docked. When you did not arrive at Gare St.-Lazare, I found that the servant had forgotten his errand amid all the distraction here today. At that point, I sent the foolish man off at once to meet you, but of course by then you'd had the

good sense to take another train."

"It's all right," I said. "I'm safe and, well, I guess I'm sound now."

"Thank heavens for that! There will be nothing further to trouble you. My wife and girls will make you comfortable at our house while your arrangements are made."

"My arrangements?"

"To return home."

"To America?" I was quite taken aback.

"Naturally," he said, looking equally surprised.

"But I only just got here!"

"To stay with your poor uncle. Tragically, that is no longer possible."

I let this sink in. Even though I'd arrived to find my uncle dead, it had never occurred to me that I would not remain in Paris. If anything, my uncle's death made me determined to stay. Someone had to find out what had really happened to him, and I had no faith in that someone being Detective Latour.

"Please, Dr. Levine," I said. "My uncle wrote me so many letters about Paris and all the things I would learn here that I would be dishonoring his wishes if I were to leave now. My parents have allowed me a year—don't tell them I ought to go straight back!"

Dr. Levine hesitated. "You really wish to remain? After—"

"I'll be all right. Honestly."

"I don't know, Paris." Dr. Levine gave careful

and lengthy consideration to a spot on the floor. At last he looked at me and said, "You are an unusual young woman. Most in your place would be only too glad to hurry back to their parents."

"If they tell me to come back, of course I will. But I don't think it's likely."

I pictured their reaction to the news. Their first instinct would be to call me home. Then they would remind themselves about broadening my horizons, and eventually they would get around to persuading each other to leave me be.

I explained all this to Dr. Levine. He found it necessary to dab his brow with his snowy handkerchief.

"I think I understand. Dear me! I hope you won't put such thoughts into my girls' heads. They have been brought up in a much more . . . well . . . traditional way."

Then he smiled and added, "But come. You have had a long and distressing day. We shall ensure that you are not fussed. A little supper on a tray, perhaps? A good night's rest . . ."

I got to my feet. "Dr. Levine," I said, trying to sound firm without seeming rude. "If you don't mind, I'd rather stay here."

"In this house? After—Oh, no, no!"

"This was always our family's house," I reminded him gently. "My father used to live here."

He sighed resignedly. "Yes, yes, of course. I do understand. Only . . . Very well. Madame

Frenais will be here to look after you. I shall call again tomorrow morning, when you are rested."

I walked with him into the hallway, just in time to see Detective Latour lock the door of a room a bit farther from the front door. I knew it must be the one where I'd glimpsed Uncle's body, just before I fainted.

Dr. Levine said something to him quietly. Latour gave me a surprised glance which turned into a frown. "Mademoiselle MacKenzie," he said, "this house is the property of your family. I cannot order you to leave. However, I must insist that your late uncle's study remain locked. There need be no guard, but I shall take the key with me." He gave me a fierce stare to emphasize the order.

"I understand, Monsieur Latour," I said meekly. "I don't want to go in there. I just want to sleep."

He nodded curtly and turned away. Dr. Levine stepped forward and raised my hand to his lips again. Then they left.

The room to which Mme. Frenais showed me was on the second floor. It was large and rather austere looking, far removed in every way from my own pretty, snug room back home. My furniture was mostly pine, covered with white lace mats and runners. Bright pictures in gleaming maple frames lined the walls. Here the furniture was green and brown and massive. There was a mirrored dressing table made of some dark wood, and there was a huge bed with a ponder-

ously carved headboard. The dark walls were bare of pictures.

As I looked around, Mme. Frenais asked if I would like to have some supper downstairs while the housemaid unpacked my things.

I told her I didn't want supper at all, that all I really wanted was to go to bed.

She showed me the electric bell to press if I wanted anything, pulled the drapes across the closed window shutters, and left me alone.

The few things I needed were in my hand baggage. After so much sea air and such a strange, sad day, I just wanted to sleep the clock round. I couldn't help yawning in the middle of saying my prayers, which I always think is dreadfully rude to God.

It was only after I'd climbed into bed and turned off the light that I remembered I hadn't said a prayer for Uncle. I sat up and said it in bed. I'm afraid I may have fallen asleep before finishing, for the next time I knew anything I was lying in bed wide awake in the pitch dark.

For a few moments I didn't know where I was. I turned on the bedside lamp and peered around the room, wondering what had awakened me. No one had come in. The drapes were still drawn, and everything looked as it had before.

The little travel clock that my class had given me as a bon voyage gift showed only half past one, so I turned off the light again and settled down. But this time sleep wouldn't come. I was wide awake.

I switched the light back on, made a cushion of pillows against the headboard, and started thinking about Uncle.

At this time early yesterday morning, he was fast asleep in his own room. A few hours later he had gotten up and dressed. Before he went to call a cab to the station, he had looked into his study for some reason, and found—what?

A burglar, according to the detective and Dr. Levine. But did burglars *really* ever wait until it was nearly daylight before breaking in? Sherlock Holmes certainly wouldn't have fallen for that, and I couldn't believe any other detective would either.

"I have trained myself to see what others overlook," Holmes had said. What would he have made of Uncle's death in a fight with a chance burglar?

Would he have believed that there *was* a burglar? Or would he wonder, as I wondered now, whether that story had been made up to hide something even more unpleasant?

Suppose the "burglar" had been someone already *in* the house—a servant, perhaps? I quickly scanned the room to be sure I hadn't missed someone lurking in the shadows or hiding behind the drapes.

Certain that I was truly alone, I suddenly became conscious of something else. I was hungry. Ravenous, in fact. I wished I hadn't turned down the offer of supper.

For a time I fought the fight of mind over

matter. Matter won. I had to eat. But I had not given up the idea that whoever had killed Uncle had been living in the house—and still was.

I slipped out of bed and put on my slippers and robe. I went to the door on tiptoe and turned the big brass knob as quietly as I could. The heavy door opened without a sound.

Peeping out, I was relieved to see that some of the electric sconces along the landing and down the staircase had been left on. I set off on my expedition to find the kitchen.

The stair carpet was thick, but the broad treads beneath it were wooden. One of them creaked sharply. I froze. Finally I realized I could not spend the rest of the night standing on the staircase. I took a deep breath and went carefully on down.

Soon I was in the hall, searching on tiptoe for the way to the kitchen. I found myself having to pass the room where the tragedy had happened. Though I willed myself to keep my eyes averted from the locked door, I couldn't.

The simple but compelling reason was that under the door there glowed a strip of light.

CHAPTER
5

I stood still and listened, but all I could hear was my own frantic heartbeat. Gingerly I moved closer, until I was right next to the heavy wooden door. Still nothing.

A keyhole cover kept me from peeking in. But I'd seen Detective Latour lock the door. If there was someone inside, then maybe it wasn't locked anymore.

Curiosity had driven away all thoughts of hunger. I was intrigued by that strip of light. Someone was in the study, and I had to know who.

I wondered what the study window—the one that had been found open—overlooked. It couldn't be the front of the house, because the

study was at the back. It was my first night in this house, and I had to think carefully before I remembered the French doors in the sitting room where I'd talked with Dr. Levine and the detective. They must open onto some back area, a situation they'd share with the adjacent study.

Could there be a courtyard? Yes, that was it! I recalled the photographs Uncle had sent, showing himself in a small rectangular courtyard. It was a good bet that his study, like the sitting room, also had French doors opening onto his prized sculpture garden.

I turned back across the hall and tried the sitting-room door, which opened easily. It was pitch black inside and I didn't dare risk any light switches. I closed the door behind me and waited for my eyes to adjust to the dark. Finally the oblong outlines of the doors began to appear dimly some distance away.

I went carefully toward them, so as not to blunder into the furniture. The French doors showed lighter and broader as I drew near. Then I found myself looking up through small glass panes at a patch of Parisian sky.

Feeling extremely pleased with myself, I groped about. Luck was with me. There was a key in the lock. I turned it carefully. The doors didn't budge. I soon found out that it was because there were bolts at the top and bottom. They slid out easily from their sockets, though. In a moment I was outside.

Sherlock Holmes would have been proud of me. I was standing in a courtyard!

It was a clear night, and by the light of the stars I could see the outlines of some statuary and a pair of urns. I stood in the shadow of the wall of Uncle's house. Farther along the wall a yellow light, softened by drawn curtains, shone through a second pair of French doors.

How about that, my dear Watson! There I was, looking at the study window. I tiptoed right up to it, supported myself against the frame with one hand, and leaned forward. There was just enough space between the curtains to glimpse the back of a dark figure bending over a desk.

Suddenly I was gripped around the waist, hard, and coarse cloth was pressed across my nose and mouth. I couldn't breathe!

A man's voice hissed close to my ear, *"Ne bougez pas!"* "Don't move!" Then he rapped on the door to attract the attention of the person inside.

The light went out immediately. Then the curtain twitched open and the pale shape of a face came close to the glass.

It stayed there for some seconds, taking in the situation. Then the door opened and my captor forced me indoors. He was holding the gag even more tightly, waiting until the other man had refastened the door and pulled the curtains shut.

The electric light came on and a soft voice exclaimed, *"C'est la nièce!"*

The awful stifling hold slackened, and I

sucked in great lungfuls of air. For a long moment I stood there, wheezing and gasping. Finally I was able to speak.

"Who are you and what are you doing in my uncle's house?" I meant to sound indignant, but my voice came out weak and shaky.

"Don't try anything foolish," said the man behind me. His hands rested lightly on my shoulders. Curiously, it was the menace in his voice that turned my fear to pure anger. Completely forgetting that he was capable of choking me to death, I began a furious tirade.

"Whoever you are, and however you got in here, you'd better—"

A soft, husky laugh stopped me. It came from the one who had moved out of sight to close the window. At first I couldn't believe what I'd heard, but as the man's accomplice came back into view, I saw that I'd been right. Although garbed in a man's velvet jacket and trousers, the second intruder was a woman—and a woman unlike any I'd ever seen.

She was tall and slender, and only a slight sallowness saved her hollow cheeks from being deathly pale. Her nose was narrow and aristocratic, her mouth rather wide and thin. But her most striking feature was her hair. Jet black, thick and curly, it sprang out from around her head like a halo—a sinister halo of writhing black snakes.

She smiled and signaled the man who still stood behind me. Then his hands left my shoul-

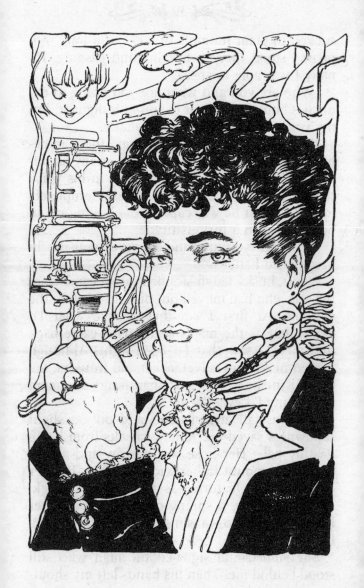

ders and I heard him slip out through the French doors. In all the time he'd held me, I hadn't once seen his face. Closing the curtains behind him, the woman turned and addressed me in flawless English.

"Forgive that hostile reception. We could not know it was you who would come."

I still do not know if it was fear or awe I felt on that first meeting. Sometimes the two are very close. "Wh-who are you?" I finally dared to ask.

"My name is Méduse. Madame Méduse. I was a colleague of your late uncle."

To my surprise she suddenly stepped forward and extended her hand. It was much whiter than mine. "Welcome to Paris, mademoiselle," she said. "May I offer you my condolences?"

The hand that took mine wore several large jeweled rings. What I noted with more interest was a striking golden bracelet in the form of a serpent. It curved around her wrist and disappeared beneath her sleeve. Two red-jeweled eyes sparkled in the light, making the bracelet seem strangely alive.

"Thank you," I said, all the while telling myself not to be overly impressed by appearances. At this point I had no idea whether she would turn out to be friend or enemy, and yet I was certain that I must not show her any fear. I decided to concentrate on getting some answers.

"How did you get in here?" I asked.

"As your uncle's associate, I have my own key

to the house and to this room," she answered smoothly. "I often work here at night. I prefer it. When everyone else is asleep or at idle pleasure, one can concentrate in peace."

"Especially with someone keeping guard," I thought, "so you won't be disturbed!" However, out loud I said, "What kind of work, Madame Méduse? Are you a doctor too?"

She shook her head. "Dr. MacKenzie saw very few patients. Research was all he cared about. We had been working together on certain projects, and all the notes are here. In view of yesterday's tragedy I brought a male escort to keep watch for me, just in case. I hope he did not hurt you."

All of this sounded pretty odd to me—but then almost everything I'd heard since arriving here had been odd.

"Then you're going on with the work?"

She shrugged. "Like life, science has to carry on through adversity."

"What are you working on?"

"Unless you were highly trained in science you would not understand if I explained."

"I might," I said. "My mother's a doctor. I'm used to scientific explanations."

"Not of this sort," she answered curtly.

"The police said no one was to come into this room," I said. "Haven't they been to see you?"

Méduse just looked straight into my eyes without saying a word. She raised a hand to

touch her hair, and the glittering red eyes of the serpent bracelet gleamed at me.

"I have been out of town all day," she said slowly. "I will go to the Préfecture when it is daytime, in case they have anything to ask me. There is nothing I can tell them, though."

"If you were out of town, how did you know of my uncle's death?"

"A friend left a message. Besides, it is in the evening newspapers."

I couldn't help a moment of admiration. What a cool customer she was!

"The detective in charge will not like it when he hears of your visit," I went on. "He will be very angry."

"I dare say," she answered. "For that reason I would prefer that you do not speak of it."

I shrugged. "I see no reason not to tell him. Everyone else has to do as Monsieur Latour says."

"All the same, I prefer that you not speak of it to anyone." Her voice had become very low, and suddenly I was frightened again. I held my tongue, wondering if she was going to threaten me or perhaps call back the man who'd seized me in the courtyard. Although the study was warm, I was shivering.

Then I realized that my gaze had become riveted to the glowing eyes of the serpent bracelet, which she was holding up between her face and mine. Although I tried, I couldn't look beyond it. It was as though those gemstones were alive!

Méduse was speaking again, and now her voice had a strange quality, as if it were an echo of itself. At the same time the serpent seemed to move closer to me of its own accord. Its eyes got bigger, boring into mine, and with a dull, sinking sensation I found I could no longer blink.

"Let me hear you promise," Méduse said slowly. "You have not seen me here. You remember nothing of our talk. You do not even remember leaving your bed. Do you understand?"

I wanted to shout no! to scream and wake the household. I could do nothing. Instead, I heard myself answer, "I understand."

As I did, my fear left me. I felt drowsy and weightless.

Méduse's voice was receding further. "We have never met. You have never seen me. Never heard my name. You know nothing of me at all."

Now I could only nod.

"Promise. Promise!"

Whether I spoke the promise or just nodded, I don't know. All I can say is that when I awoke I was in my bed and Mme. Frenais was pulling open the drapes and shutters so that bright sunlight flooded the room.

"You have slept soundly, Mademoiselle Paris?" she asked.

"Like a top." I yawned. "All night."

As far as I knew, I was speaking the truth.

CHAPTER
6

"Bonjour, mademoiselle." A pretty young maid entered the room with a big ewer of steaming water, which she poured into the washbasin. The smell of coffee was drifting into the room from somewhere beyond the open door. I suddenly realized that I was as hungry as a horse!

I thanked the maid and began to wash and dress. Toilet completed, I made my way downstairs toward the delicious coffee aroma. But in the hall I stopped short; I was outside the closed door that I knew led to my uncle's study.

Although I felt a strong urge to go in, I remembered Detective Latour's pointed warning—and the

locked door. Forgetting the coffee and my hunger, I automatically turned toward the sitting room across the hall. It was as though some force were drawing me that way.

The sitting room seemed far more cheerful this morning. The French doors that looked on to a small courtyard stood ajar. The courtyard was enchanting, open to the hazy sunlight of a mild morning. A fountain stood in its center, throwing light jets into a circular pool around it. Gold and silver fish moved under the ripples.

There were several classical statues on plinths, a pair of urns filled with flowers, and two stone benches. Three sides of the courtyard were bordered by arched passageways. A basket of bright flowers hung from the point of each arch.

Farther along the side where I stood were two more French doors. Curious, I walked over to them and found that they, too, were open.

I stepped over the threshold into a room that was immediately familiar to me, although I couldn't think why. It didn't take me long to realize that it must be Uncle's study.

There was a big desk, a tall cupboard, bookcases around the walls—all things you'd expect to find in a doctor's study. But what really caught my eye were the shelves and cabinets on the far side of the room. They held a bright array of vases, teapots, figurines, and clocks—things that I knew were part of his prized Art Nouveau collection. Some were behind glass, but many were on open display.

I examined them slowly. I had heard a lot about the collection, but although Uncle Claude's letters were filled with descriptions of his acquisitions, I hadn't really understood what Art Nouveau was or why he was so excited by it. As near as I'd been able to tell, it was a particular type of design with lots of long, curving lines taken from nature. Now, as I stood looking at the detail on a small metal clock, I saw what Uncle called its special beauty. The clock's face was surrounded by an intricate frame, and everything in it—the flowers and trees and slender, dancing vines—seemed to be intertwined, so that every line flowed into every other.

I'd have gone on looking, but my eyes had been caught by a framed oil painting over the fireplace. It was very different in style from all the other things, and I knew it at once. It had been Uncle's most precious treasure, one of Claude Monet's paintings of the Japanese bridge and water-lily pool in his beloved garden at Giverny.

Papa and Mama had raised eyebrows at each other when Mama read us Uncle's letter enclosing a photograph of the painting: "Congratulate me, my dears—I am now the proud possessor of what will undoubtedly come to be regarded as one of the finest masterpieces of Impressionist painting."

Papa hadn't thought much of it. But I'd picked up the photograph and stared at it long and hard. Even in sepia it had fascinated me. Now, seeing

it in all its glorious color, I knew why Uncle had loved it so.

Could this be what the person who had broken into the house had been after? But he'd been interrupted by Uncle and had killed him somehow. He wouldn't have dared take the picture after that.

The awful thought came to me that if Uncle hadn't had to start early to meet me yesterday, he wouldn't have looked into his study while the intruder was there. Save for me, he would have lost his treasure—but not his life!

Tears began to well in my eyes, and I think I would have begun crying if the door hadn't opened at just that moment.

"Mademoiselle!" Mme. Frenais looked very shocked indeed. "What are you doing in this room? It is not to be entered, by order of the police."

"I'm sorry, madame. I was in the courtyard and I passed the French doors and they were open. I thought I'd just like to see where . . ." As I was trying to explain why I'd come in, her expression changed from one of irritation to one of dismay.

She was standing before the open shelves, looking from object to object as though she couldn't believe her eyes.

"What is it, madame?" I asked.

"*Monsieur le docteur*—his precious *bibelots,* his *objets,* his treasures—what has happened to them?"

Mme. Frenais was holding a cigarette case with a painting of a woman's head on it. Grapes and leaves were entwined in her long hair, all in green against a dull silvery background. I couldn't see anything wrong with it.

"The colors!" she said. "They are all dulled, darkened, *d'un teint sombre*. Who has done this?"

"I think the colors are very pretty," I began. But she was talking wildly now, more to herself than to me: about how all the lovely things had been spoiled by some villain; how poor Dr. MacKenzie's heart would have been broken to see what had become of them. She wasn't crying, but there was no doubt that she was grieving. She seized one piece after another and rubbed them against her dress, then moistened her thumb with her tongue and tried to wash off the dull overlay. Nothing had any effect.

I could see now that there was a sort of yellowish look to all the enameled things, though the colors were still there underneath. I didn't know what to say, so I stood quietly as Mme. Frenais bustled around the room, continuing to exclaim with horror.

I couldn't stop myself from trying to piece together the mystery. It was understandable that the thief hadn't taken the Monet, but perhaps some of the more valuable ornaments had been taken. A lot of them were small enough to be hidden in a pocket.

I was just about to ask whether anything was

missing when Mme. Frenais suddenly swung around to face me.

"The box!" she exclaimed in French. "It is gone!"

"What box, madame?" I asked.

She went on, almost too quickly for me to understand. I managed to make out that about two months ago my uncle had come home with a small, quite plain wooden box. He had put it among the precious things as though it were valuable, and she had seen him look at it often and smile. She had never seen what was in it. Now it was gone, vanished.

"Was it here yesterday, madame?" I asked in careful French.

"How could I observe? With so many people coming and going, so much disturbance, so much distress, it was not possible to see what was here. Now it has been taken."

Mme. Frenais had not mentioned that any of the Art Nouveau things had been stolen, and I imagined she knew each one pretty well. They were all so different, not the sort you could mix up in your mind. I asked her about that. She shook her head.

"Nothing else is missing. Of course I am sure. I knew every piece as well as he did. I, and I alone, was allowed to dust them. They were my pride, as well as his. But what are you doing, mademoiselle? Please, you must not do that!"

But I'd already done it—opened one of the glass-fronted cabinets. It contained two shelves

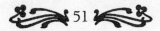

of figurines, bowls, and some jewelry pinned to velvet. I showed her what I'd noticed.

"These things aren't discolored like the others. Do you think it's because they were behind glass?"

She stared at me, then at the things in the case. I left her to take them out and peer at them one by one while I wandered about the room, looking for anything else worth noticing, as Sherlock Holmes would surely have done. But there was nothing—nothing except a piece of torn-off newspaper on the floor, half-hidden under an armchair.

I picked the newspaper up. It was only an item about a new station on the Métropolitain, the electric railway being built under the streets of Paris. What it said wasn't very interesting. What *was* interesting was the color of the paper. It was the same dull yellow as the enamels. Something made me sniff at it. There was a definite scent to it, and, now that I noticed it, that same strange smell seemed to be in the air around me.

At that moment the door to the study opened and M. Latour walked in. His expression turned positively thunderous when he saw us.

"Mademoiselle! Madame Frenais! What are you doing here? This room is strictly off-limits!"

He had spoken in French, but his meaning would have been obvious to anyone. I decided to play the innocent foreigner again and walked out, leaving poor Mme. Frenais to explain.

CHAPTER
7

I didn't know what to expect for breakfast, but I could still remember those wonderful, gigantic breakfasts at sea—everything from strawberries and melon to pancakes with maple syrup to eggs done five different ways. Even the tea, made in the proper British manner, was delicious.

But all I got on my first morning in Paris was coffee and hot croissants—pretty dull by comparison. I wondered if there would be something else to follow, but since there wasn't, I ate two extra croissants.

A newspaper lay folded on the table. I could picture Uncle Claude, seated in his now vacant chair, picking it up to read after wishing

me good morning and asking how I'd slept. It was strange how I found myself missing a man I'd never even met.

As I opened the paper, I noticed that it was printed on ordinary white newspaper stock, and this made me wonder again about the funny-smelling scrap I'd picked up in Uncle's study. I was alone in the breakfast room, so I took the scrap from my dress pocket and compared it with the newspaper. The type was the same, so it came from *Le Matin* too. But it was yellow, not white. Odd.

I put the scrap away again and ran my eyes over the headlines. I could understand most of the articles, but a lot of the news didn't mean much to me. Then something caught my eye that did:

TRAGIC DEATH OF NOTED PARISIAN SCIENTIST. Yesterday morning the body of Dr. Claude MacKenzie, well known in medical circles for his research in the field of toxicology, for which he had been awarded . . . [then followed a string of titles] was discovered at his residence in the rue Cambon. It is thought that Dr. MacKenzie's death was caused by a heart attack brought on during a struggle with an intruder. The police are making searching inquiries.

"Well, they've got about half the story," I thought. I could have given them a much more

interesting detail, about how the intruder had stolen nothing but a small, plain box with unknown contents. Then I saw that the news item had a footnote:

It is a remarkable coincidence that two other specialists in Dr. MacKenzie's field have recently met with untimely deaths in tragic circumstances. On March 10, Dr. Marc Brisson fell beneath the wheels of a Métro train as it was entering the Châtelet Station, and on March 27, the body of Dr. François Chautemps was found severely mutilated on the branch line which runs from the Place de l'Étoile to the Trocadéro. It was presumed that he had fallen from a train, though no witnesses have come forward. The deaths are not presumed to be linked. Our medical correspondent comments . . .

I didn't bother to read his comment. I knew what I thought. Maybe the deaths weren't presumed to be linked, and maybe no one had seen Dr. Chautemps fall, but it struck me as very strange indeed: two distinguished men in the same profession getting killed in the same way, and then Uncle Claude's mysterious death! Surely the police must see something suspicious in that?

It seemed likely that all three had known one another, probably quite well. My heart began to

thump madly as I made my plan. I was going to find out about the other doctors. I would discover what connection there might be between them, and maybe between the three deaths.

Now my mind and imagination were beginning to race. I slipped out of the breakfast room and hurried up to my bedroom, where I paced the carpet, too excited to sit down.

Like Holmes, I began to consider the possibilities. And no hypothesis was too wild to ignore. Perhaps there was some secret they all knew. Perhaps they'd all gotten on the wrong side of some King of the Underworld. Weren't there criminals in Paris that were called apaches after our fierce Indian tribe—villains who went about knifing people in dark alleyways and dragging their women around cafés by their hair?

Perhaps a rich, powerful man with a bitter grudge against the three doctors had hired apaches to murder them. Dr. Brisson had been standing on the Métro platform at the front of a crowd. A rough-looking man in a cloth cap had come up behind him as the train approached, and had given him a push.

Dr. Chautemps had been sitting in a Métro carriage by himself, perhaps reading. He hadn't noticed the man who had gotten in and seated himself nearby. Then suddenly he'd felt himself grasped, pulled upright, had seen a hand go out to open the door. And then—

And Uncle! Was it an apache he'd found in his

study, waiting to kill him, not to rob him? Except for the mysterious box, that would explain why nothing had been taken. Perhaps the assassin had opened it, found something he saw was valuable, and put it in his pocket. The two had struggled, and poor Uncle's heart had given out.

Well, whoever had killed those three had Paris MacKenzie to reckon with now!

I rang the electric bell and the maid appeared. I asked her to tell Mme. Frenais that I was going out.

In the twitch of a cat's whisker the housekeeper herself appeared. "Mademoiselle does not think of going out alone?"

"But of course. Why not?"

"You must understand. It is not respectable for a young girl to be without an escort in the streets."

I tried not to laugh. "Don't worry, madame, I'm quite able to take care of myself. I go out alone all the time in Chicago."

Mme. Frenais looked at me with undisguised curiosity. "Mademoiselle has no maid to accompany her?"

"Why, no. We have maids in the house, of course, and there's one who does Mama's hair and helps us look nice for parties, but she doesn't come out with me. People would laugh."

Mme. Frenais was not laughing. She was not even smiling. "Mademoiselle's uncle died only yesterday. It is not proper to leave the house so soon—and without decent mourning."

"I'm wearing my black dress," I pointed out. How could I explain that what I wanted to do was my own way of paying tribute to my uncle? Instinct told me that if Mme. Frenais knew what I was up to, she'd be even more upset. "Please, madame," I said, "I, too, am still shaken from yesterday. A walk in the fresh air would do me good."

She didn't look happy about it, but she did look sympathetic. "If you insist, mademoiselle. But please do not go too far. It is not proper." She turned to go, then added, "Perhaps in the future you will choose to have a maid to accompany you."

"Perhaps," I said to reassure her. And perhaps not. A maid to accompany me, indeed!

Moments later I was outside. That strange, foreign scent was in the air, and all along the street the window boxes were full of daffodils. Despite the awful events of the last twenty-four hours, I was eager to get to know Paris.

However, much as I already felt for my namesake city, I didn't know my way around it yet. I looked for a cab, and got one after walking for a couple of minutes. It was only when the driver asked for directions that I realized I didn't even know where the two dead doctors had lived.

The dapple-gray cab horse was well groomed, and his harness shone with brass and leather polish. I thought it was a hopeful sign, and so it proved to be. I asked the driver, in French, "Do you perhaps know the house of Dr. Marc Brisson? The gentleman who died—er . . ."

"This is a large city, mademoiselle," the driver answered. "If you want to go somewhere, you'll have to give me the address."

"But all I have is a name," I said, perplexed.

"Then I suggest you first make a stop at the Bureau Téléphonique," he said, and grinned at me. I stepped in and we set off down the rue Cambon. A few streets later we pulled up in front of an official-looking building.

"Here we are," announced the driver. I hopped out of the cab, walked into the bureau, and went straight to the desk where a young attendant sat with the telephone directories in front of her. A few moments later I was back in the cab with both addresses written on a piece of paper.

I told the driver where Dr. Brisson had lived and settled back to enjoy the sights. On my drive the day before I'd been too tired and out of sorts to notice much apart from the dazzling lights of the exposition. Now I saw that the boulevards, as I knew the main streets were called, were immensely broad, more impressive than any in Chicago. The buildings that lined them were tall, six stories mostly, and made of some kind of light stone that shone golden in the sunlight. The shop fronts looked so attractive that I wished I were on foot and could look into all of them. The pavements, which were asphalt, not stone like ours, were edged with tall, slim trees that had burst into the green of early spring.

I'd never seen such traffic—no wonder the

streets were broad! Omnibuses took up a lot of room—their drivers obviously had no intention of making their horses give way to cabs or carts or even carriages. Most of the vehicles were horse-drawn, although I saw a few fine automobiles and some motorbuses. I liked the motorbuses best. On the top decks passengers sat and enjoyed the sunshine and the passing scene. The motorbuses looked like they were more fun to ride in than the stuffy, dark little cabs (which I'd soon remember to call fiacres), and I promised myself a trip in one soon.

What fun it must be, too, to sit outside the cafés under cheerful, striped awnings and sip whatever was in those glasses. There were plenty of women and girls at the little tables, I noticed. Back home it would have been thought real fast to sit drinking beside the public highway, but here everyone seemed to do it.

My fiacre stopped, and the driver called through the trap door in the roof that we were here. I got out, paid him his fare, and looked around. I was standing in front of a house with a mourning wreath above the door. The brass plate read DR. BRISSON.

I rang a very jangly bell and waited. After many minutes the door was opened by an elderly maid. She looked at me suspiciously while I explained in halting French that I'd come to talk to someone about Dr. Brisson.

"Dr. Brisson is dead," she replied, crossing herself.

Yes, I knew that, I told her. Was there a member of the family I might speak with?

The old woman shook her head and informed me that Madame Brisson was not seeing anyone.

Carefully I composed my next speech: I had no wish to disturb Mme. Brisson. I only needed to talk to her for a few minutes. It was about something that might help her.

The woman hesitated, then indicated that I should follow her.

We climbed an awful lot of stairs. At last the maid stopped and opened a door.

After Uncle's rooms full of treasures, this one was very drab and plain, even downright dismal. Although it was the middle of the morning, the shutters were still closed. All the pictures had black crepe draped over them. A small fire burning in the grate was just about the only cheerful thing in the room. A woman dressed all in black, with a black lace veil over her head and face, was sitting by the fire, staring into the flames. Her hair under the veil was white.

The maid spoke to her quietly. Mme. Brisson turned her head and regarded me for a long moment before asking what my business was with her.

I said in my slow French, "I wish to talk with you, madame, about the sad death of your husband."

"Are you a journalist?" she asked sharply.

"No, I am Paris MacKenzie, niece of Dr. MacKenzie, who has also been found dead."

This seemed to shock her considerably. She gave a low moan and started rocking her body to and fro. Might as well get it over with, I thought, and say what I'd come to say. I went on to explain that I thought the deaths were murders, not accidents, and that I'd be grateful if we could talk about anything the deaths had had in common. Maybe as a result we could identify someone who might have had something to gain from them.

But Mme. Brisson didn't seem a bit interested. She just rocked and moaned louder, and then started crying. I'd obviously made things worse, and I felt guilty about what I'd started. I shifted uncomfortably, not knowing where to look.

The maid soon decided that for me. She grabbed me by the shoulder, yanked me out of the room, and then gave me the worst talking-to I'd ever had in my life, in French *or* English.

She made it quite clear—and I *could* understand all the words that mattered—that I was a rude, brash child who'd had the nerve to burst into a house of death and intrude on private grief. I'd shocked Madame, made her ill; *M. le docteur* was not yet cold in his grave and here I was, bothering his widow with a lot of nonsense about him being murdered. She concluded by looking at me as if I'd just crawled out of a sewer, and snapped *"Va-t'en!"* which I knew was a brusque order to get out.

Since this was obviously no time to argue, I tossed my head and stomped off down the stairs.

But I *was* awfully sorry I'd upset that old lady so. I'd only wanted to find out just how well my uncle and her husband had known each other, and whether there'd been any connection between the work each was doing. I'd even planned to try out my apache theory on her and see how she reacted to it.

But it hadn't worked out like that. How would Sherlock Holmes have handled this? Clearly, I still had a few things to learn about the fine points of conducting an investigation.

CHAPTER
8

When I was down in the street once more, I tried to decide what to do next. Since no empty fiacre appeared from either direction, I set off in search of one. I had no idea where I was, but that didn't worry me. The walk would give me a chance to see a little more of Paris.

For a moment, as I walked down the quiet, narrow street, I had the uneasy feeling that I was being followed. But I didn't see anyone, and when I emerged onto a wide boulevard, I decided it was just my imagination.

Now I was able to do what I'd wanted to do when I was in the fiacre—look in the shop windows.

And they certainly were something! Chicago had nothing like them.

The couturiers were the best. There were high-fashion frocks, big hats, and wonderful coats, many in the Art Nouveau style, embroidered with butterflies, birds, and exotic fruits and flowers. A jeweler's window was ablaze with necklaces, rings, and bracelets set with precious stones worked into elegant designs.

To tell the truth, what impressed me even more than the shop windows were the women of Paris; it was all I could do not to stare at them. Passing in their carriages or strolling arm in arm with elegant gentlemen, they seemed like beautiful birds of paradise. Even the ordinary women—clerks and milliners' messengers with hat boxes on their arms—looked chic and sophisticated. Not only were their dresses and accessories perfectly coordinated, but I soon realized that all of them, from the lowliest to the most elegant, wore paint on their faces! Their lips and cheeks were pink, their eyes were outlined in black, and their complexions had been made wonderfully pale with pressed powder. Oh, how I longed to be able to turn myself out like that!

I stopped to examine my reflection in a shop window: scrubbed American cheeks, a turned-up nose, and unstyled, rather messy blond hair. Not a bit chic, and no matter how hard I tried, impossible to imagine with face paint. Patience, I told myself, just have patience.

I walked on and became so entranced by the sights and fashions that I nearly forgot my mission, until I saw a line of cabs pulled up alongside a curb. I went up to the first cab in line, gave Dr. Chautemps's address to the driver, and got in.

This time my fiacre landed me on a broad street on one side of the great square, the Place de la République. On a stone pedestal in the middle of the square stood a bronze statue of a woman with her arm upraised—just like our Statue of Liberty.

"Gosh!" I exclaimed at the size of Dr. Chautemps's house. But at the top of the broad steps I found a plate saying that it wasn't a private house at all, but rather some sort of institute for chemical research.

Inside the entrance a porter sat in a glass box behind a counter. In a mixture of French and English he told me that Dr. Chautemps had lived in a small apartment at the top of the building. He was unmarried, and his manservant had left after his death. The apartment was locked, and no visitors could be admitted, on police orders.

"Aha!" I thought. "They've got their suspicions, after all." But that wasn't going to put me off *my* investigation. In fact, it convinced me that I was on a warm trail. But how to follow it further?

The porter must have seen me looking perplexed. "Mademoiselle might wish to speak with Monsieur Fleury," he suggested.

"Monsieur Fleury?"

"Monsieur Marcel Fleury. He is a student who worked closely with Dr. Chautemps."

"Oh, that would be just fine. How do I find him?"

"He is in the building now—most likely in the late doctor's laboratory." The porter banged a big brass bell on his desk. "The boy will take Mademoiselle there."

A very small boy in uniform emerged from what I had imagined to be a cupboard behind the desk. The porter instructed him and the boy led me away, through many bewildering corridors filled with chemical odors.

At last we stood before a door with a frosted glass window. The boy rapped his knuckles on the door, a man's voice called *Entrez!* and I was shown in.

"Mademoiselle MacKen*zee*," the boy announced formally, before marching out and shutting the door. Across the room I saw a dark head peering into a microscope.

The room was quite like our chemical laboratory at school, only with fewer benches and chairs. But it wasn't the layout that held my attention: it was the very tall, very young, *very* good-looking man who was crossing the room to greet me.

My immediate impression was that he wasn't many years older than me—twenty, he looked at most. He had a neat, dark mustache, pale skin, and rather rumpled curly black hair. His white lab coat was rumpled, too, and that was the only thing that saved me from feeling like a nervous twelve-year-old. Anyone who wore a rumpled lab coat had to be human, no matter how good-looking he was. I suddenly realized that he was the first young Frenchman I'd met.

"Mademoiselle MacKenzie?" he was asking as he came to a halt before me. I saw puzzlement in his eyes. "A relative of Dr. Claude Mac-Kenzie?"

It didn't escape me that he had given me the benefit of any doubt by speaking English. I thought that was an elegant sign of finesse. Imagine an American boy volunteering to speak French!

"The *late* Dr. MacKenzie's niece," I replied. "From the United States. My name is Paris MacKenzie."

His eyebrows went up a fraction at hearing my unusual name, but he was too well mannered to comment on it. He made a sharp little bow and held out his hand for me to shake.

His expression and tone were serious as he spoke again. "Permit me, mademoiselle, to express my deepest condolences upon your tragic loss."

"Thank you, monsieur. But I only arrived yesterday"—how long ago it seemed as I said it!—"and I never had a chance to meet my uncle. I guess perhaps you knew him better than I did."

He shook his head. "I was introduced only

once, by Dr. Chautemps. It was at a conference some months ago."

That was a disappointment to me; and there was another coming in his answer to my next question.

"Were they close—my uncle and Dr. Chautemps?"

"To my knowledge, not at all. I believe their only acquaintance was at public functions."

Without stopping to think whether it was the right thing to do, I found myself asking, "And Dr. Brisson?"

I noticed a spark of surprise in the dark eyes, followed by what I took to be a look of understanding. But once again he shook his head.

"Dr. Chautemps never met Dr. Brisson. I asked, after the tragedy, whether they were friends. Dr. Chautemps said they were not."

"Isn't that odd?"

"The scientific establishment in Paris is very large, mademoiselle. I have already asked myself the question which I believe is on Mademoiselle's mind, but no answer has come."

It seemed I'd run up against another blank wall; but at least I'd found someone whose thoughts seemed attuned to mine, and who was willing to talk about them. He offered me a chair, which I accepted gladly.

"Now, mademoiselle," he invited when we were seated facing each other on the straight-backed laboratory chairs. I'd already decided that I could trust him, so I went into my story, leaving nothing out. When I'd finished he was silent for a long moment. Then he met my eyes with his serious gaze.

"Forgive me, mademoiselle, if I say I do not know how I can help you. But you see how difficult it would be to prove any connection between these three tragic deaths, or even between the three victims."

I must have looked very dashed. He said gently, "You understand that everything about them would have to be examined from years ago. Their methods of work, their private circumstances, everything. I do not think Mademoiselle could do this. It is work for the police."

Of course it was. Somehow I'd imagined that the lives of all three scientists would be an open book, that the people who'd lived or worked with them would know all about them and be willing to give me the information I needed. Faced with this serious, sensible young man, I began to realize how impulsive I'd been. Sherlock Holmes, indeed! Life wasn't a detective story in which clues conveniently turned up. For the second time that morning I felt like a fool.

I saw that he knew what was going through my mind, and what he said next confirmed it.

"Mademoiselle MacKenzie, a thousand pardons. I have said what I should not. It was very clever of you to think of this connection, and perhaps you should make more inquiries. But . . ."

"Yes?"

"In your place I should go to the man who might tell you what you want to know. There is a Dr. Levine, a close associate of your uncle's—"

"But I met him last night!" I exclaimed. "He's been very kind. He asked me to stay at his house with his family."

Marcel Fleury's brow cleared, and he smiled for the first time. His grave features seemed to light up from inside, and he looked handsomer than ever.

"Then of course you must go to him," he said. "What a fortunate thing that you have met so soon."

The only difficulty, I told Marcel, was that I didn't have Dr. Levine's address with me. He said that was not a problem and fetched a directory from a shelf.

Moments later, after Marcel had found the address, he escorted me to the ground floor. He was quiet on the way down, but as I turned to leave, he spoke abruptly. "It is almost the hour when I break my studies for *déjeuner*. Lunch, that is. Would you care to take some food with me, mademoiselle? There is a very good café just across the street."

"I would love to," I answered truthfully, "but I can't. Madame Frenais—that's my uncle's housekeeper—will be worried that I've been out so long, and I still have to see Dr. Levine." I could have kicked myself as soon as I said it. Now, I told myself, he probably thinks I'm a child. Besides, he probably only asked me to lunch to be polite.

It was Marcel who drew me out of these dire thoughts. "If you should ever need my help, mademoiselle—if there is anything at all—you can find me here," he said, handing me a visiting card. I couldn't help smiling. An American boy his age would never have carried such a thing. The French had such polish!

Marcel pointed out the direction I should take, warning me that it was a long way and that I should take a fiacre. I said I would, but I didn't. I wanted to find my way around more of Paris before I returned home.

I started to walk along the Boulevard du Temple, but I got tired of its everlasting length and turned off onto a narrower, older street. The shops there were mostly curiosity shops, full of the most fascinating old things—pictures, jewelry, figurines, books.

At last I tore myself away and went on. What I didn't notice was that the little street led back to the Boulevard du Temple, and that when I reached it, I mistakenly turned back to the way I'd already come.

By the time I'd realized this, I was quite lost and my feet hurt, and the sights around me were rapidly losing their novelty. I kept trying to hail a fiacre, but every one I saw was engaged. The boulevard was busier than before and seemed far noisier. It was at this moment of exasperation that I saw a most inviting sight: a Métro station.

I'd never traveled by underground railway. I had no idea where to go in order to end up anywhere near Dr. Levine's. But now was the ideal time to find out!

I found the ticket window and asked for the station nearest to Dr. Levine's address. The clerk told me that it was at the end of the line. I got myself as far as the platform and sank down on a bench.

It was a strange feeling, being underground. The bright electric lighting and the newness of everything made it seem like another world. I heard a rumbling in the dark tunnel, and a strong gust of air made me clutch at my hat. A train appeared, traveling the wrong direction for me. It stopped long enough for a few passengers to get off on the opposite platform, and then it rumbled smoothly on its way again.

The passengers vanished through the exits. There was no one else on my platform. Yet I had a strange feeling that there *was* someone. This was the second time I'd felt like someone was keeping track of me—following me. Again I told myself the idea was nonsensical. Who would follow a complete stranger in Paris?

Just as I was thinking this and wondering whether I ought to have gone straight home to rue Cambon instead of chasing off to Dr. Levine's, I heard a rush of feet. Before I could turn around, an arm was flung around my neck and a very strong, very rough hand was clamped over my mouth.

CHAPTER
9

I twisted and turned desperately. It flashed through my mind that my attacker meant to throw me onto the track, as Dr. Brisson had been thrown, and I struggled even harder. My head must have struck his chin, because he cursed and took his hand away from my mouth. That was all I needed. I opened my mouth wide and gave the loudest, longest, most unladylike scream I could manage.

The man grabbed me again, but he was too late. There was a clatter of feet on stone stairs and then someone was dragging him away. Whistles were blown, men were shouting, and at last I was free, though I was gasping for breath. I saw two gendarmes dragging off a roughly dressed man bent nearly double, with his arms forced up behind his back.

Then two more gendarmes were on either side of me, going on excitedly at me as though the whole affair had been my fault!

When a train came rushing out of the tunnel and drew up at the platform, they told the driver to take us straight to someplace called Hôtel de Ville, and bundled me into a car. I wasn't sure that I liked rattling along in semidarkness inside a small, drably furnished railroad car. And the burly men in uniform on either side of me were certainly no comfort. I tried to speak to them, but either they didn't understand my French or they just weren't bothering to answer. Neither of them said a word.

We whizzed through several stations, leaving people staring at our car from the platform. At last we slowed down and came to the Hôtel de Ville Station. The gendarmes got up and practically dragged me out of the car and up a lot of steps to the open air.

At least I recognized where we were. Rearing up above smaller buildings were the twin spires of the Cathedral of Notre Dame. I had no chance to appreciate it, though—my two escorts led me part of the way across a bridge onto a big island in what I knew was the river Seine.

"Where is this?" I asked the one who seemed to be giving orders.

"*Île de la Cité*," he condescended to answer for once. "*Préfecture de police.*"

The building they were leading me toward was huge and daunting. Gendarmes stood on guard outside the main doors, and many more were bustling about in the vaulted vestibule. I was led straight through some swinging doors into a long corridor that reminded me of the chemical laboratory, but without the smells. And *that* reminded me of Marcel Fleury and made me wish he were with me now.

After many more corridors and stairs, enough to make my knees ache, I was escorted into an office. Like everything else about this building, it was big, with a big desk between the windows and a big man sitting at it. He was in uniform, with extra braid and important-looking insignia and some medal ribbons. These and his gray hair and beard made me wonder if he was the chief of police in person. I couldn't think why he should be interested in me.

He didn't smile or stand up to receive me. He listened while the senior gendarme gave him some rapid details of what happened, then abruptly motioned me to a chair before the desk.

I was aware of the other men in the room at desks of their own. One had been using a type-writing machine but had stopped when we came in. Although I didn't look around, I could feel them staring at me, and I knew I wasn't looking good. My hair was coming down, I was hot, my legs were aching, and I badly wanted to wash my face where that man's hand had been clamped over it.

The gendarme who had been with me all the time began to repeat in a stilted, formal way, "*Cette mademoiselle anglaise . . . se promenant toute seule . . .*" He added this time how he'd rescued me singlehanded from my attacker.

"Excuse me," I interrupted in English. "Maybe you'll let me say something."

The chief looked startled. I knew he'd understood what I'd said, though the boastful gendarme and his companion were looking blank.

"I am American," I went on. "This is my first day in Paris and I've been followed and attacked. No one warned me that it was a dangerous place *or* that your police don't care two hoots about what happens to people who get into trouble they didn't cause."

The gendarmes looked from me to their chief, then at me again. They probably expected an order to drag me down to a cell to cool off. Instead, the man behind the desk addressed me in careful English.

"Mademoiselle, it is obvious that you are a newcomer to France, or you would know that it is customary to give persons their title. A superintendent of police merits at least the courtesy of 'sir' or 'monsieur.'

"Furthermore," he went on, "I am surprised that no one has instructed you that it is not *convenable*—proper—in France for a young lady of your station in life to walk about the streets unaccompanied."

"Yes, I have been told," I said. "However, back home in America a girl is free to come and go as she likes."

"This is not America, mademoiselle. This is Paris. No doubt all you see here are fine boulevards and expensive shops. But there are dangers here, and you should be aware of them. Behind the hill of Montmartre, for example, live a whole colony of people whose homes are crude huts, shanties. *Voyous*, they are called. I do not know how it would be in English, but they are as savage as wolves. They prey on respectable people going about their innocent affairs in the city; especially foreigners, whom they can recognize on sight."

"Was it one of those who attacked me . . . monsieur?"

"A typical one, from my constable's report. The Métro is already well known as a place where unwary travelers can be robbed before help comes. It is a public danger, this Métro. It should be closed down, not extended."

"Well, I'll be careful next time," I said. "Can I go now?"

He was astonished. "Go?"

"What else is there, monsieur? You've warned me what a dangerous place this is. You have the man who attacked me, and you've locked him up safely, I trust. Oh, and I'm grateful to the officers for rescuing me."

I smiled at the two men, who were listening uncomprehendingly.

The superintendent stared hard at me, sighed, and then seemed to relax. "Jérome," he ordered one of the other men in the room, "fetch coffee for Mademoiselle."

The superintendent turned back to me, and I was glad to see that his expression was less severe. He didn't actually smile but he gave me a little nod, which I thought was meant to reassure me.

"Mademoiselle," he said, "you must understand our position. By wandering the streets of Paris alone you make it much harder for the police to protect you—and you give every encouragement to the *voyou*. If you want our help, we must first have your cooperation.

"Now, Mademoiselle will also appreciate that it is necessary for us to take down a few particulars. Even against so obvious a villain, we still need to make a case."

I nodded, finally understanding why I had been brought here. Then I thought that since I was being interviewed by a senior policeman, I might as well make the most of it.

"Monsieur," I said, "pardon me, but I did suspect I was being followed earlier. I had walked quite a distance and I felt it long before I entered the Métro."

He nodded, smiling. "The sharp instincts of youth," he said patronizingly. "It is a common method of those wretches, the *voyous*, to mark a

victim and follow her or him until the right place
and moment comes. They have all the time in
the world. An entire day spent in someone's
footsteps is profitable indeed if there is a purse
full of money, a jewel, or a watch to show for it.
You, mademoiselle, are alert enough to have felt
someone following you, but you never would
have spotted him. It bears out my warning not
to walk alone."

The coffee came and I was beginning to feel
friendlier toward the superintendent.

"I—I didn't think it was anything like that," I
said.

He frowned again. "You believe you may have
been followed for some other reason?"

"Maybe. You don't suppose someone else
could have been trailing me around, and the
attack by this—this *voyou*—happened as a coincidence?"

"But who would be following you? And why?
Mademoiselle, I think it would be well for you
to tell me the full circumstances of your being in
Paris." He then drew a sheet of paper from a
japanned stationery holder and unscrewed the
top of a fountain pen.

"As a rule, the task of taking down a few brief
particulars would be that of a duty constable,"
the superintendent said. "In this instance, mademoiselle, I shall make it my personal concern—
and pleasure."

I could have laughed. Papa had told me how
Frenchmen could switch on the charm to order,

and Mama confirmed it. Whether the police superintendent was sincere or not, I couldn't tell, but a willing ear in an official quarter was just what I needed.

"Well, my name is MacKenzie. Paris MacKenzie," I began.

He had started to write, but suddenly broke off. He glanced up, his face expressionless, and asked, "Any relation of the late Dr. Claude MacKenzie, mademoiselle?"

"He was my uncle," I replied. And then I told him everything that had happened since my arrival in Paris.

CHAPTER
10

The superintendent questioned me for what seemed like hours. When I finally arrived back home that afternoon in a cab hired by the police, Mme. Frenais ordered me to bed at once. I didn't argue. The events of the last two days had taken their toll. I could feel myself shaking, inside and out, and there was no strength left in my arms and legs.

"Mild shock," pronounced Dr. Levine, who arrived not long after I'd gone to bed. "A natural reaction. I shall instruct Madame Frenais to keep you in bed for two days, young lady."

"Dr. Levine—" The effort to speak was almost beyond me.

"It would be better if you were to stay quiet. Superintendent Lebois telephoned to give me full details of what happened. Dear me, if only you had told them who you were at the outset. And if *only* you had not insisted on going out alone like that!"

"But did he say he believed me—about Uncle Claude's death and those others? There *has* to be some connection."

"Just open your mouth a little, my dear."

I obeyed and he popped a thermometer into it, effectively silencing me.

"Mademoiselle Paris," he said warningly, "I wish you to put all such speculations out of your mind. I am going to give you a mild sedative and Madame Frenais will repeat the dose at intervals. The more sleep you get during these two days, the sooner you will be well again."

"Nnnnn!" I tried to protest. He ignored me.

"I have received a cablegram from your father."

My heart thumped. Would I be ordered back home immediately?

"He requests that I arrange for you to represent him at his brother's funeral," said Dr. Levine. "There is to be no inquest to delay it, so it will take place on Thursday. Unless you rest properly, you may not be fit to attend, which I am sure would disappoint your papa. You don't want to alarm your mama and him with news that you were too ill to go, do you?"

I shook my head. He withdrew the thermometer from my mouth but gave it only a cursory glance and didn't find it necessary to shake the mercury back to normal.

"But—" I began. Dr. Levine held up the thermometer again in a mock threat and his eyes flashed me a warning.

"I was only going to say, Doctor, that I don't have to go back home, do I?"

"Nothing has been said so far. On the other hand . . ."

"Oh, please!"

"I will make a bargain with you," he said. "If you promise to stay in bed and rest and take my medicine, I shall report nothing about the scrapes you have managed to get into. Agreed, Mademoiselle Paris?"

"D'accord, Monsieur le docteur."

I kept my side of the bargain. I wanted very much to do as Papa wished and attend Uncle's funeral, but most of all I wanted to sleep. So I took the sedative from Dr. Levine and enjoyed the feeling of drowsiness it brought on. Sleep, when it came, was welcome.

On the morning of the day before the funeral, Mme. Frenais surprised me by carrying in my breakfast tray herself. I saw a big, broad-brimmed cup of coffee, a plate of croissants kept warm inside a napkin, and a dish of fruit conserves and jams.

"Dr. Levine has instructed that if Mademoiselle feels able to face these, then she is cured," the housekeeper said with a smile.

"Consider me cured," I replied.

After breakfast the maid, Lucille, came to tell me that my bath water had been drawn and that she would put out my clothes. When I had dressed and gone downstairs, feeling entirely refreshed after my long rest, I found a small, chic woman awaiting me in the sitting room. There were several large cardboard boxes around her chair.

Mme. Frenais introduced her as Mme. Vaupin, a milliner friend. Although Mme. Vaupin put on a show of deference toward me, I could see her looking my American black dress up and down with something less than admiration.

She spoke no English and communicated with me through Mme. Frenais while she opened her boxes. From among the tissue-paper sheets she produced three black hats with black veils, several pairs of black gloves, and two black parasols. I was to choose accessories to go with my black dress for the funeral.

I tried on the three hats and chose the second. I knew instantly, from the faint click of the milliner's tongue against her teeth, that she didn't approve. At her bidding Mme. Frenais invited me to put on the first hat again. Mme. Vaupin made a deft adjustment to the way it sat on my head and stood back satisfied. As I examined my reflection I *thought* I could see why this hat suited me better, but I couldn't have said why.

I got the gloves wrong, too, and resigned my-

self to the same thing happening with the parasols. So I pointed to the one I liked least and was
congratulated with an eager nod and smile from
Mme. Vaupin. I was beginning to formulate my
own rule: If I think it looks terrible on me, it's
probably *très chic*.

After lunch I rested in bed again and read my
one and only piece of mail. Muriel Hooper had
sent a short letter asking if I'd arrived safely and
telling me how exciting her conference was. She
had met several famous psychics, and had at-
tended a seminar on the pyramids that left her
nearly delirious with joy. But her letter ended
on a disquieting note: "Do be careful, Paris. I'm
sure everything will turn out for the best, but
see that you think things through as carefully as
your friend Mr. Holmes would."

Dr. Levine came to call late in the afternoon
and, after a brief examination, pronounced me
well. I was allowed up for a quiet evening—on
strict orders not to go out of the house or do
anything more strenuous than begin the long
letter home which I intended to finish after the
funeral. An early night and a sound sleep without a sedative completed my recovery from what
the doctor referred to as "an overrapid accumu-
lation of shocks" to my system.

He called for me early the next morning. I
was already in the sitting room, turning this way
and that before the mirror, trying to figure out
why the milliner had insisted on this particular
hat, and what it was about the way I'd been

shown to wear it that made the hat exactly right.
Perhaps, I thought, she had wanted to make sure
that I bought the one that would be the most
difficult to wear properly. Dr. Levine's arrival
cut short this unworthy speculation.

"Splendid, my dear!" he exclaimed. "Permit
me to say that you wear your clothes with a
natural grace. If only my own dear girls . . . But
we should be getting along. Any delay would be
most unfortunate."

Dr. Levine, who was wearing an immaculate
frock coat, a black cravat, and a glossy top hat,
gave me his arm and we walked out to his au-
tomobile, which waited beside the curb. The funeral wreath on our front door and the black
ribbons on the huge maroon motorcar had attracted a few staring bystanders. I thought back
to the other crowd which had been on our steps
so recently, and it was like recalling a bad dream.

The doctor helped me into the back seat and
sat beside the chauffeur in the front. Before long
we arrived at the Church of St. Pierre de
Montmartre, which was small and ancient and
dark. Candles lit the chapel, and the smell of
incense was nearly suffocating.

Dr. Levine and I were among the first there,
and since I was the only family member present,
we were seated at the front of the chapel, just a
few feet away from the coffin. I don't know why
seeing the coffin should have shocked me so—
perhaps because it made me remember the body
I had seen the first night I arrived in Paris.

I heard others filing into the pews but resisted the temptation to look around. A priest, robed in grand vestments, began to chant in Latin. We knelt and prayed and a choir sang. It was not easy sitting in that pew, but at last the service ended. The coffin was carried past us by the undertaker's men. Dr. Levine patted my hand and indicated that I should be the first to follow it. To be honest, I was glad when he caught up with me and gave me his arm to lean on.

The burial was to be nearby in the Cemetery of Montmartre, so we walked in a procession out of the church and into the blessed sunshine.

A short time later we assembled around the waiting grave, and I was at last able to see the faces of everyone present. Detective Latour was standing opposite me. He gave me a respectful nod. There were several other men, mostly elderly and formally clothed. I guessed from the way they greeted Dr. Levine that they were all scientists or doctors.

A taller, younger man stood deferentially behind them. It gave me quite a start to recognize Marcel Fleury. Considering that he didn't really know Uncle, I'd never have thought to see him here. I didn't ask myself why he'd come or why it should make me feel good, but it did.

Beside Marcel, Mme. Frenais stood sobbing, holding a handkerchief under her veil. I recognized the middle-aged man beside her as much from his gray livery as from the one glimpse I'd caught of him back at the house. He was Uncle's

chauffeur and valet, Hector, and he was every bit as emotional as Madame. It seemed they were representing the staff, for there was no Lucille and no one I could imagine to be Hector's wife, our cook, whom I'd not yet met. "Uncle must have been very good to them," I thought, and suddenly I wondered what would become of them now. I hoped that Uncle's will would in some way provide for them.

The coffin was lowered. I cast a handful of earth onto it from a silver scoop that the priest handed me. The earth hit the coffin with a sound of finality that shocked and distressed me. I looked away, to the scene spreading out below us, and realized that the city my uncle had loved so dearly was now lost to him forever. Then, for the first time since I had arrived in Paris, I cried.

We bowed our heads for the final benediction. As the priest spoke, something made me raise my eyes. There was another mourner across the grave from me—someone that I hadn't noticed before. She was a striking figure, tall and elegant in her mourning clothes. She stood at the back of the small group, slightly apart from everyone else.

As I wondered who she could be, a breeze disturbed the lower half of her veil. Her hand went up to draw it down in place, and as it did I caught sight of a bracelet that seemed to coil up her forearm like a golden serpent. A pair of ruby-red points flashed in the sunlight. In a moment they were gone.

Although my glimpse was momentary, I knew I had seen the bracelet before. But where? And when?

CHAPTER
11

When the funeral was over, Dr. Levine and I started back to his house to have lunch with his family.

We were turning onto the Boulevard de Clichy, just downhill from the cemetery, when we overtook a closed carriage. The shades were open and I noticed a woman's arm resting on the window frame. Once again I stared at that strangely familiar serpentlike bracelet.

This time Dr. Levine was sitting next to me in the back of the car. "Dr. Levine," I said, "do you know who that tall woman at the funeral was? The one standing all alone?"

He sighed. "Ah, that one," he

said, and turned away to look out of his window.

"You know her, then?"

"Oh, yes, yes." His vagueness made me more curious.

"She was wearing a remarkable bracelet," I said. "Made like a snake coiling around her arm. It even had stones where the eyes would be—rubies, I think."

"Hah!" Dr. Levine fidgeted with the top hat on his knees. Then he turned to me and said heatedly, "That thing is a symbol of her character. If you could see her without her veil you would understand why. She *is* a serpent by nature—even by name! She is called Madame Méduse."

"You mean—she's kind of poisonous?"

"*Poisoned*—infected with the venom of jealousy and frustration. She claims to be a scientist herself!"

"Claims?"

"Science is a male profession," he said gently. "Women do not belong in it."

"My mother's a doctor," I pointed out.

"Oh, yes," Dr. Levine allowed. "There are a few female *doctors*. Some of them are very able, I understand. Higher scientific research is quite another matter, though."

I could just imagine Mama tearing into him over that remark. How could such a nice man be so pompous?

"But this Madame Méduse claims to be a real scientist?" I said.

"Yes. Of course, anyone with a smattering of chemistry and physics can make a claim like that. Being recognized by the scientific institutions is quite another matter."

"And she isn't?"

"Her talents are what one might call eccentric. She is one of those rebels who persist in questioning and challenging things about which other scientists agree. Such people refuse to accept what their elders and betters know, from long experience, to be the truth."

"But isn't that how new discoveries sometimes are made? When someone steps over the limits to try out some new idea?"

Dr. Levine sighed and patted my arm.

"Ah, Paris, my dear, it is good to hear a young person speak so. Your poor uncle would have been pleased. Between ourselves, I agree with you. I believe it will not be long before we hear of some woman achieving great things. There is one here in Paris now, called Marie Curie, who experiments alongside her husband on what is termed radioactivity. Mark my word, if they achieve important results her name may be renowned equally with his."

I mentally withdrew my charge of pomposity. "But why not Madame Méduse, then?"

He hesitated, turned his hat around by its brim a couple of times, and then went on, although in a lowered voice.

"Please do not discuss what I shall tell you, Paris. The fact is, what Marie Curie is trying to

do is intended to benefit mankind. What Méduse is after is not."

This was becoming more and more intriguing.

"How do you know?"

"There are times when scientists need to consult with one another. To compare notes and even seek advice. You understand?"

"You mean that's what she's had to do?"

"Precisely. To put it simply, she is seeking a collaborator."

"To help her work something out?"

"To get her a hearing, more precisely. She has approached the scientific institutions, even government departments, but no one will listen to her. None of them have ever listened to a woman before, so none are prepared to be the first to risk it. Imagine the position of anyone who agreed to sponsor a woman's discovery if it proved a disaster! He would be the laughing-stock of the scientific world."

"But if it wasn't a disaster?"

"Well, that is another matter. Meanwhile, Méduse knows that her work will be seriously considered only if a respected member of the profession—a man, that is to say—draws attention to it on her behalf."

Suddenly I thought I knew why she had been at Uncle's graveside. "Do you think she approached Uncle Claude for that sort of help?" I asked.

"I know she did," he said. "He told me she had requested an appointment."

"Was he planning to help her?"

"Definitely not!"

"Just because she's a woman?"

"No, no. Your uncle was not the sort to be prejudiced like that."

I was glad to hear it. "Well, then, why wouldn't he help her?" I asked.

At this point the car pulled up in front of a large, elegant house. Dr. Levine shook his head and put his hand on the door handle.

"Do you think she *has* discovered something?" I said.

"From what your uncle told me, she claims to have made a discovery of great importance to our country," he answered. "Both your uncle and I could only speculate about what it might be, knowing her lack of scruples."

The chauffeur was coming around to the door on my side. "Please say nothing to anyone of what I have told you," said Dr. Levine. "I must ask you to promise."

I did. But it wasn't going to stop me from thinking—thinking and wondering about Uncle and Mme. Méduse.

The house door had opened. Stout Mme. Levine and her two skinny daughters, all wearing black frocks and solemn expressions, were waiting to receive me.

I guess I was looking solemn, too, and not solely because I had just come from Uncle's funeral. I was thinking about Mme. Méduse and trying in vain to place her. She had asked to see

Uncle. Did that mean she had been to the house?

The house! But no. No picture would form.

"Mademoiselle MacKenzie! Welcome at last! These are my girls, Rachel and Rebecca."

Mme. Levine was speaking English for my benefit and the girls were curtsying deeply to me, eyes correctly cast down. I gave my best little bob in return and forced myself to concentrate on being sociable.

CHAPTER
12

The lunch at Dr. Levine's was a long, dull affair. He had hinted to me that his daughters weren't exactly vivacious, and that proved an understatement.

In any case, Mme. Levine held forth for much of the time, commiserating with me repeatedly about Uncle's death and my own unenviable position. What, she asked, was to become of the house, the servants, and myself?

I couldn't have told her, even if I'd wanted to; I hadn't given the house and servants much thought. Fortunately, Dr. Levine commented that Uncle's will would take care of those details when it was read in a few days' time. The

household would carry on as usual in the meanwhile, and I was not to worry about money matters. As executor of Uncle's will, Dr. Levine had made financial arrangements through Mme. Frenais.

I felt secure enough with my allowance from Papa, and just hoped that I would not be summoned back home—it was a possibility I did not like to consider.

The rest of lunch was not much better, so I was grateful when, late in the afternoon, I was at last able to tear myself away.

Dr. Levine sent me home in his car but excused himself from accompanying me. I guessed that he wanted to avoid more questions about Mme. Méduse.

The doctor had prescribed an early night for me, and for once I was happy to obey. I badly wanted that day to be over.

I awoke early the next morning feeling refreshed and clear-minded. In fact, the first thing I did was sit up in bed and begin to review all that had occurred since my arrival. As I thought about my meeting with Mme. Frenais in the study, I remembered something I'd forgotten entirely: the yellowed scrap of newspaper—the scrap that seemed to be connected to the dulled Art Nouveau ornaments. And since I was thinking clearly for what felt like the first time in days, I promptly had an inspiration. Marcel Fleury and the Institute for Chemical Research! Of course, I'd thought about him quite a bit, but

not about what he did, so it had never occurred to me to ask his opinion of my one solid clue.

I would go to the institute this morning, straight after breakfast, and bring the paper and maybe one of the ornaments with me. He could test them right away.

On second thought, I decided as I bustled to get dressed, I shouldn't burst in on him again. "Never pop in on people, and don't let them do it to you," Mama had told me. "It's an intrusion, either way."

Perhaps I could telephone him there? No, that would be just as bad. I'd have to write a letter.

So I sat down at the writing table and began scribbling. Then I checked myself, crumpled up the paper, and started again on a fresh sheet. This time I made myself go slowly in my best hand. I admit it. I wanted to impress him, not just ask for his help.

For one thing, in the first version I'd addressed him as "Dear Marcel." But that wouldn't do. He was "M. Fleury" until, if ever, he invited me to use his Christian name; it would have been shockingly fast of me to assume intimacy when I hardly knew him. Finally, I wrote down *"Cher Monsieur Fleury,"* and decided that it looked just right—not stiff, yet not too forward, either.

I kept the letter short, saying that I'd come across something odd which might be connected with my uncle's death. It seemed to be "of a chemical nature"—I thought that sounded im-

pressive—so I wondered if he could perhaps advise me?

I hurriedly finished dressing and slipped out to mail the note in the *pneumatique*—an underground system of air-pressure tubes that whisked messages throughout the city.

I had sent my note early, so there was plenty of time to get a reply the same day—if he *did* reply. Marcel might not be at the institute to receive my letter. Or he might be there, but so busy with his microscope that it would be hours before he'd even read it. Or maybe he'd read it and toss it aside with a quiet laugh at a gauche American with pretensions about a matter "of a chemical nature." Maybe . . .

Marcel's reply came right after lunch. He was busy at the institute all day, but if I could visit him there late in the afternoon he would most willingly discuss whatever was perplexing me.

I had a tactful but direct talk with Mme. Frenais before I left the house. I explained that while I appreciated her concern for me, I was quite able to take care of myself, and she really had no cause to worry about my acting like a lady. I was wearing proper mourning and wasn't going to do anything to bring disgrace on the name of MacKenzie. She in turn replied that she knew I hadn't had an easy time and was only trying to spare me additional discomfort, but since I seemed bound to do as I pleased anyway, would I please be careful? I was beginning to grow very fond of Mme. Frenais.

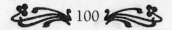

This time I took a fiacre all the way to the institute. No more Métro for me—by myself, anyway—and no more exploring the streets without a map.

Marcel came down to the lobby to meet me. He was still devastatingly handsome. "To the laboratory," he said with a smile.

"First, I want to thank you for attending my uncle's funeral yesterday," I said.

He blushed and looked at the floor. "It was nothing, mademoiselle."

He escorted me to a small laboratory—not the one I'd visited before, but another one along the same corridor. The benches were covered with scientific equipment—glass pipes and rods, tubes, microscopes, bowls, and beakers. There was no one else in the lab.

I opened the discussion. "Well, here it is—My Great Clue. It's probably nothing at all, just a scrap of paper I found on the floor in my uncle's study the day after his death. I thought perhaps some French newspaper used this color newsprint."

Marcel took the scrap, examined it, sniffed it. "No newsprint is colored this way. No, this has been soaked in something. Let us have a look."

He placed the scrap on a slide under one of the microscopes and peered at it.

"The discoloration is certainly caused by some chemical. I can't say which one at this moment, but we shall experiment."

He carefully tore off a piece of the paper,

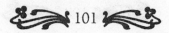

mostly blank margin. Then he poured some water into a shallow enamel bowl and floated the paper in it. We watched. A faint yellow stain began to spread into the water and Marcel nodded, as if in approval. As we continued to watch, the yellow stain paled, then vanished. The water was now colorless, but the newspaper still had a yellow tinge.

"As I thought," Marcel said, "it is the result of a chlorine derivative. You see how it has decomposed into hydrochloric acid and oxygen?"

I didn't, but I was very impressed. "The stain hasn't gone from the paper," I commented.

"No, but do you notice it is changing? There is a shade of purple in it now. I find that very interesting."

I watched as he added other things to the bowl of water—a pinch of powder, a drop or two from a glass pipette. Then he went to a large book and consulted it. At last he shook his head and shrugged.

"It is nothing I know. I suspect that the stain was caused by a gas, which under atmospheric pressure . . ." It was impossible to follow the string of terms and figures that he reeled off. I just listened.

Then I said, "There's something else." I told him about the discoloration of the enamels on the Art Nouveau objects in Uncle's study. "And what's more, I've got one here." I removed from my purse the cigarette box Mme. Frenais had been so distressed about.

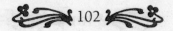

Marcel took it, touched it, then brushed it lightly with a piece of cloth dipped in clean water.

"This baffles me," he said. "The substance of this box is not porous, yet the stain has sunk in and seems indelible. I have never seen anything like it. What a pity. It is such a fine object."

"There was something else," I said. "The only thing that seems to be missing from the study as a result of the burglary is a plain little wooden box. Nobody knows what was in it. Do you suppose it could have been something to do with this?"

"Wooden? Unlikely. One does not store chemicals in wood. Mademoiselle, I'm beginning to fear I've failed you. I don't seem to have any answers to your questions."

Impulsively I said, "Please don't call me mademoiselle. My name is Paris."

"I had noted your name when we first met, mad—Paris. We pronounce it 'Paree,' of course, but your way is charming. I have never heard it used before as a feminine name. Yet your *nom de famille* is MacKenzie." He pronounced it with more difficulty. "That is American?"

"Scottish. But I'll tell you all about that—sometime. Isn't there anything else we can do to follow up my clue?"

Marcel pondered. "I am not sure how much of a clue to anything it is. But whatever has caused this metal to lose its color must be very strong and therefore very dangerous—poisonous, even."

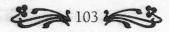

"Do you know anyone who *could* trace this chemical?" I asked.

Marcel grinned. "I can think of one person—my friend Paul. He is a fellow lodger with me in the Quartier Latin. He's a more advanced student than I am, but I'm afraid he's quite lazy." He glanced at the clock. "Do you want to go and see him now?"

"Oh, yes! And the Latin Quarter—isn't that where all the artists and the models are, and the night life?"

"Not much night life at this hour, I fear. But it's worth seeing at any time, la Rive Gauche."

"That's the Left Bank of the Seine?"

"Yes. It is the true Paris—more so than the great boulevards and squares. They have been built for show. The Quartier is the real thing—shabby, sometimes disreputable, but genuine."

I looked at him, again thinking how different he was from all the boys I knew at home.

"You're a very serious person, Marcel."

"Am I?" For the second time I saw him blush. "In what way?"

Now I felt embarrassed. "I only meant you seem to really love this city."

He thought for a moment. "There's a great deal here to love. You will see. In time you will feel the same way."

"I hope so," I said. "A lot of me belongs here."

He regarded me with interest and a certain amount of amusement. "You will have to tell me all about that."

Laughing and feeling suddenly bold, I stood up and headed for the door. *"Bien sûr, monsieur. But you will have to take me to the Latin Quarter first!"*

CHAPTER
13

We left the institute on foot, but Marcel said that we had better take an omnibus, since we had quite a distance to go. The nearest 'bus stop for the route we needed was a long way off. As we walked to it, that uneasy feeling of being followed came back to me. Call it sixth sense, maybe—but I was almost certain that we weren't alone.

I remembered reading a detective story that gave very specific directions on how to spot a shadow: Don't look back, but keep stopping to look in windows for a reflection of whoever is behind you. If you spotted the same man this way three or four times, you could bet your bottom dollar he was trailing you. A woman shadowing you was said to be less easy to detect than a man, because women stop to look in windows more often. So the theory went, anyhow. I tried putting it into practice after we'd turned onto a boulevard where there were plenty of shop windows.

After the first couple of stops I was considering several suspects. One by one, though, they passed us by: a nursemaid pushing a baby carriage, a boy carrying a basket of long loaves, a gendarme on patrol, a hawker of miniature toys.

The feeling of being followed persisted, though, and I stopped at yet another window. I could sense that Marcel was getting curious. I'd been all eagerness to go to the Latin Quarter, yet here I was window-shopping!

"I'm sorry, Marcel," I said. "You'll think I'm imagining things, but I have a feeling someone's following us."

He was polite enough to take me seriously, and turned for a long look at the crowded street.

"Don't do that!" I squeaked. "You never let on that you know they're following."

He looked astonished at this—beginning to wonder, I suppose, what sort of odd creature he'd gotten himself mixed up with.

"Sorry," he said as we moved on. "But whether you are imagining things or not, never mind, there's our 'bus."

The omnibus had just pulled up at the curbside. To my extreme relief, no suspicious-looking person followed us on board. We sat on

the open top deck so that I could watch the city below, and at last we were on our way toward the river and its bridges.

"Now," Marcel said, "you promised to tell me how you came to be named after the city."

"Well, it all began with Captain Jamie MacKenzie in the Napoleonic War," I explained. "The French family he was lodged with at Chantilly after he'd been captured bore him no hard feelings. They only wanted France to enjoy peace again."

"Like so many," said Marcel. "Why we put up monuments to Napoleon, a Corsican lout who brought our country to ruin, I will never understand."

"Well," I went on, "there were two young daughters in the house. The story goes that both set their caps for the dashing Scottish captain. He'd gladly have married both, but decided on the elder one, Antoinette."

"Perhaps they spun a coin for him," Marcel teased.

"He married her when the war was over," I continued. "And that's how I came to have a Scottish grandfather and a French grandmama."

"It's a romantic tale." His voice was serious again. "Your grandfather returned to Scotland?"

"No. The Captain, as we always call him, was quite a good painter, but he'd seen that the best way to make a living from art was as a dealer. So they moved here to Paris and he founded the Galerie MacKenzie."

"I've heard of it. It wasn't far from here," Marcel said. "But it's gone now."

"Right. Our family left in 1870, when the Franco–Prussian War wasn't going France's way and it was obvious that Paris would be occupied. The Captain reckoned it was time to look toward a new country—the United States."

"And your father was his son?"

"Yes. Father was born and brought up in Paris and began studying law here. When they moved to Chicago in '74, it was only three years after most of the city had been burned down in the Great Fire. They'd rebuilt a lot of the city, and it kept growing, so there were lots of opportunities for real estate agents and lawyers. Papa finished qualifying in Chicago and went straight into a good partnership."

"The typical American success story."

"With bells on—wedding bells, at that. Mamma says it was love at first sight, or first hearing. Papa's accent bowled her over."

"And you?" Marcel asked. "Are you also charmed by the French accent?"

"Not after growing up with it," I lied.

"I see," he said, trying to conceal a smile.

"Marcel," I said impulsively, "I *can* speak French if I make the effort." He looked at me, and I realized how tactless I sounded. He must have thought I meant his English wasn't very good.

"Sorry," I added quickly. "I didn't mean it like that." In my anxiety to reassure him I patted his forearm, which I guess could have seemed very fast of me. I quickly withdrew my hand and stumbled on: "What I meant was that, since I'm supposed to be practicing French, I wonder if you'd mind if I tried it out on you?"

He surprised me by laying his hand on *my* arm and saying, in a formal way that managed to sound rather droll, *"Chère mademoiselle, j'accepte votre aimable invitation avec grand plaisir."*

All I could think of to reply was a weak *"Merci, monsieur."* But we laughed together, and so came a little closer. From then on we talked a mixture of French and English, in line with what I could manage. And bit by bit, I found my confidence growing.

As we crossed the Seine through the Île de la Cité, Marcel gestured toward the buildings on either side of the broad roadway.

"Police headquarters and Sainte-Chapelle, the old palace-chapel."

"And Notre Dame," I was able to put in. "I've seen it already." I didn't add that I'd seen the Préfecture, too—from the *inside*!

We were soon across the island and into what Marcel told me was the Boulevard St. Michel. "This is the Paris I love," he said. "It is a different place. The other side is so formal and pompous. Over here—well, see what I mean?"

We had made a stop at the end of a side road. There were stalls filled with flowers in every color of the rainbow, and fruits and vegetables piled so high on their pavement barrows that

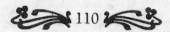

they threatened to spill over onto the ground. The women in this neighborhood market were bareheaded and dressed in brightly colored blouses and skirts. Buyers and sellers gestured animatedly over the produce; I could hear their rapid chatter even from inside the bus. This must be the local news and gossip exchange, I decided—the equivalent of our corner grocery store back home.

"Oh, look!" I pointed to two swarthy-skinned young men wearing striped shirts, loose neckties, and broad-brimmed hats. "Are those apaches?"

I thought Marcel suppressed a smile, but he said, "Possibly. You meet all sorts in the Quarter."

The bus moved on. The road became narrower and the shops on either side smaller. I smelled cooking. Some men and women stood in a cluster around a trestle table, spooning something from bowls held close to their mouths. A stout woman was stirring the contents of an iron pot hanging over a charcoal brazier.

"Onion soup," Marcel said. "So thick that the spoon can stand up in it. It is a meal in itself."

Now we were passing a group of small restaurants and food shops. Long sausages hung in rows in the windows, along with shelves filled with bottles and enticing arrangements of food. I thought there really must be something wrong with my French when I tried to translate the shop names.

"Le Chat qui Rit—The Cat that Laughs?
"L'Escargot Bienvenu—The Welcome Snail?"

"*Exactement!*" exclaimed Marcel. "So long as it makes people smile and gets remembered, that is all that matters."

"Oh! And what are those?"

There was a group of shops with cuts of raw meat on display. The signboards only showed what I supposed were their owners' names, but each shop had the carved head of a noble-looking horse over its doorway.

"*Boucheries chevalines,*" Marcel answered. "They sell horsemeat."

"Ugh!"

All the same, I was falling under the spell of this colorful, pungent-smelling neighborhood, whose people looked so unconventional and easygoing.

"This is it!" Marcel exclaimed as the 'bus lurched to a stop.

We pushed our way through the noisy throng on the sidewalk and onto a series of narrow cobblestone streets.

We must have gone about half a mile, and I had completely lost track of where we were as Marcel led me through a labyrinth of winding alleys.

"Here we are," he said at last, stopping in front of an extremely dark little alley. A doorway was just visible in its gloom.

"You'll have to tread carefully. Some of the stairs aren't to be trusted."

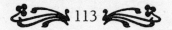

"You go first, then," I said.

"It's better that you do," he answered. "Then I can catch you if you stumble."

"What have I gotten myself into now?" I wondered, and stepped into the darkness.

CHAPTER
14

There were several flights of stairs, interrupted by short landings with closed doors at their sides. From behind the doors came a variety of sounds: a violin playing, a baby crying, two women quarreling shrilly.

The stairs ended at a landing with only a single door. Marcel reached past me to push the door open, revealing one large room. It was unexpectedly light because a lot of the angled ceiling was window.

A man's voice called a cheerful greeting, and I saw that he was at work on a canvas propped on a tall easel. The man was short and beanpole thin, with a drooping black mustache and straight black eyebrows that slanted up to points. He would be in his early twenties, I guessed.

"A new model for me, Marcel?" he asked. *"Bonjour, mademoiselle. Enchanté de faire votre connaissance."*

He gave me a sweeping bow, holding out his palette in one hand and his long brush in the other.

I returned a greeting in French, and Marcel said, "Mademoiselle MacKenzie, may I present my friend and roommate, Stéphane Carrel?"

"Ah, so this is the Mademoiselle Paris you have told me of!" cried Stéphane in English. "He might at least have said he was bringing you here, mademoiselle. We're a little behind with our housework, as you can see."

I could indeed, but the higgledy-piggledy clutter of the place was like a romantic dream come true. This was exactly how I'd always imagined a bohemian atelier in Paris.

The bare wood floor was stained with splotches of paint. Canvases were propped against a wall, and books and magazines overflowed on shelves. I noticed small sculptures, plaster models of a foot and a pair of crossed hands, a small wooden figure representing a human body, with jointed limbs. There were wine bottles and glasses, a guitar, pipes and a tobacco jar . . .

A round iron stove obviously doubled for heating and cooking. A griddle, a frying pan,

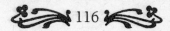

battered saucepans, and a skillet hung from hooks, along with strings of onion and garlic. Tins and stone jars lined a shelf, interspersed with pieces of apparatus for chemical experiments. I guessed that the plain square sink and faucet, like the stove, were used for both cooking and experimenting.

"Where's Paul?" Marcel asked Stéphane.

"Just slipped out to the tobacconist's. Ah, here he is now."

Paul came lumbering into the room, red-faced from climbing the stairs. Tall, heavily built, and obviously a few years older than the others, he bent over my hand in an aristocratic manner when Marcel introduced us.

"Enchanted!" he exclaimed.

"So now you have met my fellow tenants," Marcel told me. "Stephane, as you can see, is an artist—or so he likes to think. Paul is a medical student like myself."

"What they term a mature student," Paul said with a grin. "I began at medical school some years before Marcel, but I find it agreeable there, so I stay on and on."

"He's too lazy to work for exams," Stéphane commented from the easel.

"Too afraid of qualifying," Paul corrected. "In that event, my rather rich parents would insist on buying me some dull practice far from Paris and my friends. I intend to make my studies last as long as possible."

I could see his point. This was a style of Pa-

risian student life that I'd read about and envied: the sort of thing I had pictured enjoying myself after a few months with Uncle had given me the confidence. I'd never thought of myself as a painter, and I didn't fancy studying medicine, but there had to be something I could do for a living while sharing an atelier like this with some other girls.

"In order to prolong his studies," Marcel told me, "Paul has worked in more departments at the institute than almost anyone, so he is acquainted with experts in every branch. That is why I suggested bringing our problem to him."

"What's this? A problem for me!" Paul exclaimed, rubbing his hands together comically. He turned serious, though, when Marcel brought out the discolored scrap of paper and the faded Art Nouveau cigarette box. Stéphane came over to look at them, too, while Marcel repeated my story of how the ornaments in Uncle's study had been mysteriously affected.

Paul sniffed both objects, then hunted around the room for something. At last he found it—a microscope—lying on its side on a heap of magazines. He rubbed the eyepiece with his sleeve, then used the miscroscope to peer at the cigarette box and the paper in turn.

"Well?" Marcel asked him.

Paul shrugged. "The microscope tells us nothing. If, as you say, the things protected behind glass weren't affected, then there must have been some vapor in the room which did not reach them. Was your late uncle in the habit of doing experiments there, mademoiselle?"

"I don't know. Where would the vapor have come from?"

"It could have been in a bottle," Paul answered. "It would have had to be very powerful indeed to have an effect like this."

"Not to mention the effect on the doctor's lungs when he took the stopper out," said Marcel.

"Quite. One would think he'd have corked it up again as soon as he got the first whiff."

"Unless," Marcel said, "he'd dropped the bottle or knocked it over, and the liquid, or whatever, spilled out."

"Then he would have run out of the room— fast," Stéphane added.

"Suppose he couldn't," I said. They stared at me. I was thinking aloud. "What if a single sniff was enough to make him unconscious? Or what if someone had taken the bottle there, *meaning* to use it?"

"Who, someone jealous of his collection?" said Marcel. "You think they intended to ruin it?"

"I think they went there to use it on *him*!"

There was a moment's stunned silence.

"To *kill* him?" Marcel gasped, looking incredulous.

"Surely they would have killed themselves as well," Stéphane pointed out.

"No, no," Paul corrected him. "They would

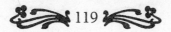

have gone prepared, with some sort of protection."

"And left quickly by the French doors as soon as they were satisfied the potion had worked," I said. "If they'd gone out by the study door, the fumes would have gotten into the rest of the house." I turned to Paul. "Marcel hoped you could tell what chemical affected the paper and the box by analyzing them."

"It's no ordinary acid or spirit, that is certain. I'd guess it was something specially blended."

"But you can't tell positively?"

Marcel heard a note of impatience in my voice.

"I only said that Paul would know of the right person to approach," he reminded me.

"What about the police?" Stéphane asked innocently.

"Do you think they want to be bothered when they have it all sewn up tidily?" I snapped. "A straightforward heart attack—no need for an autopsy or inquest. And that's it, as far as they're concerned!"

Paul held up a hand to stop me. "I understand your frustration, mademoiselle. What I was going to suggest was that you should take these objects to a private analyst. He will give you a certificate of his results, which you can then wave in front of any policeman's nose, and hint that if you don't get action you'll take your story to the newspapers. Then you'll see them move!"

"That's brilliant, Monsieur—"

"Paul. Paul, Marcel, and Stéphane. Your per-

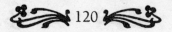

sonal Three Musketeers, at your service at any time, mademoiselle."

"Paris," I insisted firmly.

"Make it Four Musketeers," said Marcel as I shook hands with Paul and Stéphane all over again.

"I know the very man for you," Paul said once all the handshaking was done. "His name is Vigny. I'll write down his address—it's quite near the Arc de Triomphe. He's a wizard at chemical analysis, and his name is respected in the police courts. Whatever his findings are, they'll have to believe them."

"Can you spare the time to go there with me?" I asked, but Marcel cut in quickly.

"I'll take you. You must allow me to escort you home, anyway."

It was only then that I realized how dark it had become. The big sloping window showed the gloom of evening falling over the city.

"Isn't it late to call on him now?" I asked Paul.

"It's never too late for old Vigny," he answered. "He is always in his laboratory. He considers sleeping a waste of time."

"Come on, then, Marcel," I said. "Let's go!"

CHAPTER
15

We left our omnibus in what Marcel said was the avenue Kléber. Right ahead of us was something I recognized at once, the great towering bulk of the Arc de Triomphe.

Marcel said, "Another monument to that Corsican lout. Napoleon stamped himself all over Paris."

We walked a little way before turning off onto a quiet street of tall, narrow buildings. They looked as if they had once been houses; now there were business nameplates on every doorway. We found the one reading DR. CHARLES VIGNY and went in.

A young woman was standing behind a desk covered with papers.

Her coat and hat lay ready, and from the way she was arranging the papers I guessed she was ready to go home. She looked doubtful when Marcel asked to see Dr. Vigny, but disappeared through a doorway, to return a few moments later and invite us through.

We went into a plainly furnished waiting room. The young woman wished us good evening and went out, closing the door just as an inner door opened and a tall, thin, gray-haired man came in. He wore a white laboratory coat and had a pince-nez perched on his prominent nose.

"Vigny," he introduced himself with a little bow to me.

Marcel introduced us and explained that we were trying to discover why certain objects in a room in a private house had become mysteriously discolored. He said nothing about Uncle's death, and Dr. Vigny gave no sign of recognizing my name. Marcel handed him the cigarette box and the scrap of paper.

Dr. Vigny turned them around in his hands, rubbed them, sniffed them, and then said, "If you will kindly take a seat, monsieur, mademoiselle, I will conduct a few tests. They should not take long."

He indicated the wooden bench against the wall, and went away again through the laboratory door.

"So," I said, "we wait and see. Did you think he looked hopeful?"

Marcel shrugged. "If there is a perfectly inno-cent explanation, do you still propose to con-tinue trying to find out more about Dr. MacKenzie's death?" he asked.

I'd already asked myself that same question and hadn't been able to answer for sure.

"Perhaps," I replied. "Perhaps not. Maybe I'm imagining too much, and the police are right. Although they do have some strange ways when it comes to doing their job."

Marcel smiled. "You'll discover many more things that are strange, compared with Amer-ica."

"I don't see how things could get much stranger than they've already been," I said.

He looked at me, suddenly shy. "Am I strange to you?"

"You're different from the boys back home," I admitted, "but in a nice way. Come to think of it, though, you are very mysterious, Monsieur Fleury. You've told me almost nothing about yourself."

"Ah, there is so little. No dashing Scottish captains in my family. My father is a farmer near Arles. That's in Provence, in the southeast."

"I've heard that Provence is very beautiful."

"It is," he said. "Also very historic."

"Do you have brothers and sisters?"

"Three brothers, two sisters. Do you?"

I shook my head. "I don't mind. I guess I like being the only one. Do you miss them?"

"Yes, I do. We are a very close family. I never

needed to bother making friends outside, so I find it difficult to do so here in Paris."

"Paul and Stéphane are good friends, aren't they? I like them."

"So do I. We have some enjoyable times together. Only I . . ." He broke off and then glanced at his watch. "Dr. Vigny doesn't seem to be getting any results."

We must have been sitting there for a quarter of an hour. I hadn't really noticed, except for hearing the chemist's voice a little while back. He seemed to be addressing someone rather loudly, perhaps an assistant.

"I expect he'll be through soon," I answered. We talked some more about our homes and families. Another fifteen minutes passed with still no sign of Dr. Vigny. Finally I said, "I really ought to be getting back home—I mean, to rue Cambon. It's quite dark and I don't want the housekeeper getting in a fuss and telephoning Dr. Levine."

Marcel got up. "I'll ask the doctor how much longer he'll be."

He went over and rapped on the door. Sure enough, we heard Dr. Vigny call out that he would only be a few more moments longer.

"He could at least send his assistant to see what we want," I said.

"If he has one."

"I thought I heard him talking to someone a while back."

"I heard that too," Marcel said. "I think he was speaking on the telephone."

"I never heard it ring."

"I'm sure he was telephoning, from the way his voice was raised."

"Why didn't he finish attending to us first?"

"Perhaps he needed to tell his wife he'd be home late," Marcel said with a grin.

"Paul said he practically lives here," I pointed out.

"Well, something else then."

Marcel went to the laboratory door again, and I followed. We put our ears to the door and listened. Almost immediately I heard Vigny's voice, this time sounding as though it was being kept deliberately low. The tone was unmistakably angry. I caught the words, "How much longer?" and then, "It had better be soon." There was the sound of a telephone receiver being replaced.

Marcel beckoned me away from the door, putting a finger to his lips. "You heard that?" he whispered.

I nodded. "It sounded like he's hurrying someone to get here."

"Or someone else is already on the way, and he's getting anxious. He was checking up."

"The police?"

"Could be."

"Oh, not *them*!" I groaned. "I didn't tell you that they had me down at the Préfecture once already. They kept me for ages and asked me all sorts of horrid questions. Anyway, why would he send for them?"

"Perhaps he's found something suspicious and thinks they should be told. Paul said he works with them a lot."

I was furious. "He's got no right! He should consult us first, before everyone starts jumping to conclusions."

I marched to the laboratory door and thumped on it with my fist. "Dr. Vigny!" I called. "Please come to the door."

"Very shortly, mademoiselle," came the agitated reply.

That did it. "I'm getting out of here now," I said. I turned the knob on the outer door and pulled. Nothing happened. I pushed with a shoulder, but the door stayed shut.

"It's locked too!" I told Marcel. "He's got us locked in!"

"But he can't know the other door's locked. It must have happened when the secretary left."

"Well, he probably knows by now!" He couldn't have helped it, the way my voice was raised.

I suddenly realized that even if he'd heard every hysterical word, Dr. Vigny couldn't see us. I turned to face Marcel, put a finger to my lips, and pointed to the window.

Marcel understood instantly and we tiptoed across to it. It was a sash window; Marcel tried it and we saw that it was going to open without trouble. He looked at me inquiringly. I nodded. I had no intention of waiting here meekly until the police came with more of their blustering

questions. Whatever Dr. Vigny's suspicions were, we hadn't done anything wrong, and I didn't intend to spend half the evening trying to make them believe that.

Marcel raised the window silently. I hoisted my skirts up knee-high and threw one leg over the window sill. Marcel hastily looked the other way as I climbed out, and then he followed me.

In a moment we were standing on the sidewalk of a narrow street. No one was in sight. At one end I could see lights, vehicles, and people. The other end looked quieter. I grabbed hold of Marcel's arm and we set off quickly in that direction.

We hadn't gone far when a figure loomed up in front of us, blocking our way. He was tall and burly and in the faint light I saw the gleam of uniform buttons. Police!

There wasn't time for us to tell each other to try to look natural. We knew what to do, and slowed down to a saunter. I even leaned my head on Marcel's shoulder, hoping the gendarme would considerately give way to a couple of sweethearts.

He didn't. He stopped walking toward us and made a movement with his arm. I couldn't help giving a little cry when I realized that he had taken out a small pistol and was pointing it at us.

I was even more astonished by what Marcel did. He threw himself forward and collided with the policeman, who was so taken by surprise that he reeled back a few paces.

"Quick!" Marcel cried to me. "The other way. Run!"

But my feet wouldn't move. I was petrified by what he had done. To strike a policeman just because I didn't want to be bothered answering questions! Now we'd both be in real trouble.

"Run, Paris!" Marcel shouted again.

I still hesitated. Then it was too late. The gendarme had gotten his balance back and was leaping at Marcel.

There was no time for Marcel to fend off the attack. I saw a flash of metal, then a thud as the gendarme brought the pistol down on Marcel's head.

Marcel crumpled to the ground and lay deathly still. I stooped down next to him, horrified.

"Marcel!" I cried. "Oh, Marcel!" He didn't move.

I stared up at the bulky, uniformed figure standing over us.

"What have you done?" I demanded. "He wasn't really attacking you. We would have come with you!"

He bent toward me and grabbed my arm so hard it hurt.

"You *are* coming with me," the man said savagely. "Start walking—and if you try anything clever you'll get what he got."

He was proposing to leave Marcel lying there senseless!

"But—" I began to protest.

He wrenched my arm behind me, and I groaned in pain. I was helpless.

He pulled me toward the darker end of the alley.

CHAPTER
16

I stumbled along in that agonizing grip for what seemed like hours. One dark alley led to another and another after that. For a while we were on a dimly lit street, but I couldn't recognize it, and soon we were back in the alleys. In all that time we never passed another living soul.

Finally he pushed me into a dark entryway. I could just see some iron latticed gates. He rummaged with his free hand, and I heard the jingle of keys as he unlocked the gates. He slid them back, and when we were inside he shut them again and clicked a padlock. Then we were going down stone stairs, and I was trying not to trip.

To my surprise we came out at last onto what could only be a Métro platform. A few electric lights were on, but there were no people about. I saw stacks of building materials and pieces of machinery, and it dawned on me that this was a section of the line that was still being built.

There was a train standing on the tracks, but it wasn't the passenger type I'd traveled in before. It was a single car, obviously designed for transporting workmen.

The man knew exactly what he was doing. He pulled me along to the little train and shoved me aboard. Before letting go of me he drew out his pistol with the other hand. I took the hint. When he loosened his grip I just sank down on the nearest seat, which he indicated by a jerk of his head. I wasn't planning on trying anything. I was just hoping my arm wasn't permanently damaged!

He took the driver's seat and expertly started the train. As he did so, headlights came on, piercing the darkness ahead, and we were off. He turned to me, grinning nastily. And suddenly I realized he was the gendarme I'd seen patroling behind Marcel and me earlier that afternoon. He'd been following us all day!

I was sure this was no ordinary gendarme. Much as I didn't care for the Paris police, I had to admit that it was not their style to knock an unarmed man unconscious and then kidnap a young girl at gunpoint.

I studied the man's face, and my heart sank.

Not only was he not a gendarme, he was a *voyou*—the very man who'd attacked me in the Métro!

The train moved on, but after only a minute or two the man pulled on a lever which brought the train to a halt. I saw that we were beside another unfinished platform with a sign saying BOISSIÈRE. The man waved his pistol, indicating that I should get out. Another flight of steps was in front of me, and he shoved me roughly toward them. He was right behind me, and I didn't even think of trying to escape.

Halfway up the stairs was a small door. He told me to halt there and to knock. I did, and after a few moments the door opened. My escort prodded me forward, and I found myself in a brightly lit room. The walls were shiny white, and there seemed to be very little in the way of furnishings.

The woman who had opened the door was tall and slim, and dressed entirely in black. She looked familiar, and then I realized why—she was the mysterious "mourner" at Uncle's graveside, Mme. Méduse! Any doubt in my mind was erased when she raised an arm toward me and let her sleeve fall back. There was the coiled serpent again, with its glittering ruby eyes!

I stared at it—and there was a kind of "click" in my mind. Suddenly it seemed as if all the pieces of a jigsaw puzzle were tumbling together to form a complete picture.

The picture was of the woman in black, her

black hair like little writhing serpents, standing in Uncle's study. Then I knew that the man had been there as well, but my memory of him wasn't nearly as vivid. It was the woman who seemed etched in my mind. And now something else came back—the words of Muriel Hooper's strange prediction of "misfortune brought about by a woman."

Madame Méduse saw me recognize her, and her pale lips smiled. I knew before she spoke how her voice would sound; husky and even a bit mannish.

"It is *so* good of you to come," she said. "Do sit down."

"I'd rather stand," I snapped back to show her I wasn't going to be bossed around. In fact I was scared—very scared. My arm hurt terribly, too, and I'd have been glad to sit down. The "gendarme" settled it for me by pushing me onto a straight-backed wooden chair.

"Tell this bully to keep his hands off me," I said. "Look what he's done to my arm!"

I pulled up my sleeve to show her. The marks of his grip were an angry scarlet. She came forward to look at them and gave a hiss of disapproval, then turned to the man and began abusing him in rapid French.

I was glad that she'd addressed me in English, which had made me answer in it automatically. She couldn't know that I understood French, and I resolved to keep it that way. My pretended ignorance could prove very useful.

"He hit my friend over the head and left him unconscious in the street," I added, hoping it might fuel her anger against this thug, who was obviously under her command.

It worked. Méduse's voice sharpened as she reeled off a string of furious invective. The poor man's defense was quite interesting. It seemed she had sent him to Dr. Vigny's in answer to Vigny's telephone call. The man was to pretend to be a gendarme and, through some elaborate story, convince Marcel that I alone was to go with him to the Préfecture. Of course it didn't turn out that way.

"He attacked me first," the man explained in an aggrieved tone. "Just flew at me, so I had to hit him in self-defense."

I nearly cried out that it had been a deliberate savage attack on Marcel, but I held my tongue, not wanting them to know I understood what they were saying.

"You should at least have summoned Vigny to give the boy aid," Méduse said to him.

The man shrugged. "I dared not linger. Someone could have come. The girl might have run off. Your orders were to bring her here alone, at any cost."

Mme. Méduse waved him away angrily, and he moved to the doorway. I could see that he was resentful and humiliated and aching to take it out in violence against someone. Between a savage like that, and his scheming, unstable female boss, I knew there lay danger for me. For

the moment I was in their hands. I'd have to pretend to play along with them.

Mme. Méduse turned to me again. "I am so sorry, my dear," she murmured. "My man here—he is my bodyguard, by the way—admits that he acted hastily and a little too violently toward your friend. It was partly misunderstanding, partly accidental. It is certain that by now your friend will have recovered or been found, and I can only offer my apologies for what happened." Then, in a suddenly bitter voice, she went on, "You see to what sort of lengths I am driven! When they conspire to deny me recognition for my work, these men, they do not pause to consider that they make an enemy of one who is worth any half-dozen of them!"

"Enemy? Conspiracy?" I echoed innocently. "I don't know what you're talking about."

"Listen to me, Paris, my dear." She sat down and took my hand; it was all I could do not to pull it back. "I am a scientist, the equal of any in France. For years I have worked very hard at my research, and finally I have made a discovery beyond anything known to the scientific world. I do not exaggerate when I tell you it could change global politics. Do you follow me?"

I nodded. Méduse's voice was calm, but in her eyes there was an unnatural brilliance.

"Naturally," she continued, "it is of the utmost importance that work of this sort be recognized. However, in this country, unlike yours, there is a conspiracy among the men of

the scientific community. They are so afraid of women that they will not even look at the research a woman has done! For years they have shunned me, but this will not go on. I have sworn that no matter what it takes, my work will be made known. They cannot stop me any longer."

"Well, I guess I understand the way you feel," I said, trying to sound calm. "But what does any of this have to do with me?"

"You can help me. I know you can. Help me, and we shall be great friends."

"And if I don't," I thought, "what an enemy you'll make!"

"Help you in what way, Madame Méduse? I'm not a scientist. I'm just visiting, and I hardly know anyone."

"You know Dr. Levine well enough. Speak to him on my behalf. Persuade him to become my sponsor."

"Why me? Couldn't you approach him yourself?"

"Do you imagine I haven't? He won't listen any more than the others would."

Others? Could it be true, then, that Uncle *had* been one of them, and that when he'd turned her down she'd . . . !

Méduse added to that suspicion by hastily trying to cover up. "I mean, of course, male scientists in general. I have implored so many, but invariably they have rebuffed me."

I couldn't come right out and accuse her of

taking revenge against Uncle and those other two doctors; but that was the way it was looking to me now.

I shivered. It was certainly chilling to realize what my situation was. I was almost certain that the obsessed woman sitting before me had at least some connection with Uncle's mysterious death. And I was her prisoner—in a secret, underground lair!

I had only one advantage: she seemed desperate for my help. I knew I had to play on that for my own safety—and maybe even to discover the truth behind those murders.

I said, "I suppose there wouldn't be any harm in my trying to persuade Dr. Levine to help you, Madame Méduse."

"None at all!" she interrupted eagerly, her eyes glittering. "I knew I could convince you in spite of the clumsy way this blundering fool brought you here!"

"Perhaps," I went on carefully, "you should tell me what you want Dr. Levine's support *for*. It might be easier to persuade him if I knew what I was talking about."

She looked startled, and then she regarded me intently for a time. Dr. Levine had hinted that Méduse was up to something undesirable. If I could find out what it was it might give me the key to other mysteries.

"Very well," she finally said. "But I must warn you of the consequences of betrayal, either by Dr. Levine or yourself."

"I understand," I said. "What do you want me to tell Dr. Levine?"

What she proceeded to reveal was horrific and mad—but all too real, as I soon found out!

CHAPTER
17

"As I told you, I have made a great discovery," Méduse said with a triumphant air. "It is one which will benefit the nation—and, of course, our allies, including the United States of America. I have discovered a vapor that can render anyone who inhales it unconscious."

I'd expected something far more dramatic than that. "So can chloroform and ether," I said.

"My vapor is different, many times more potent. Also, it acts instantly. It can be carried anywhere in small quantities, in jars or small canisters—in soldiers' knapsacks, for instance. Now do you see?"

"You mean it could be used against an enemy."

"Exactly! Soldiers equipped with my gas containers would need no other weapons, only masks to protect themselves from the fumes. Instead of shooting bullets and shells they would project the canisters. Their enemies would be overcome. By the time they recovered, their positions would be overrun and they themselves disarmed—a bloodless victory!"

"It wouldn't kill them?"

"Most would come around again within minutes," Méduse went on. "What matters is that they would have been unconscious long enough to be overpowered." Méduse made a dismissive gesture. "A few might die—those with weak lungs, for example. But after all, someone has to die in a war."

Now I knew exactly what Dr. Levine had meant about Méduse. He had described her as "poisonous," and it was no exaggeration. She was planning to poison entire armies!

"Armies don't use gases like that in wars," I said in what I hoped was a level voice. "I'm sure neither America nor France does."

"Not yet," she replied calmly. "Which is why the first to do so will conquer all before it. That is what makes my discovery of such great importance. If only those fools had recognized that! Those narrow-minded old men!"

Suddenly the connection was all too terribly obvious. Méduse had murdered my uncle with the very gas she was describing! I fought to control my emotions. "Pretend you're Sherlock

Holmes," I told myself, "and take this step by step. Draw her out. Force her to confess."

"I can't believe they're all like that," I said aloud.

"That, my dear, is only because you are still very young. You will soon learn that all men are fools."

"There was one who would have at least listened to you," I said, guessing that Uncle Claude had had a change of heart and had agreed to hear Méduse out after all.

"Oh, yes, he listened," she raged. "Listened and told me he didn't want anything to do with my project. And he paid, as they will all pay."

Suddenly she stopped, realizing what she'd just said. She stared at me, her eyes narrowing with defiance. When she spoke again her voice had regained its icy calm. "It was an accident, Paris. You must believe that. He would be alive today if only he had cooperated."

Now I didn't care what I was saying or what might happen to me. "So you did kill my uncle!"

" 'Killed,' if you like. Not murdered. It was a complete accident, believe me. I had an appointment to visit him that evening, to discuss the possibility of his helping me. He had refused to see me once before, but then agreed to hear me out that night. I took a bottle of the vapor with me. When I explained my ideas he became increasingly angry. He said he wished nothing to do with warfare. I am afraid I became agitated and accused him of male prejudice against me, like the others. He banged his fist on his desk, where the bottle was standing. It fell on to the floor and the stopper came out. It was on his side of the desk, so I could do nothing to save him from the fumes without risk to myself. I made my escape."

"And you didn't go back?"

"I did not dare," she said. "I had no protective mask."

"But you came back the next night—when I found you. Why?"

"To search for the bottle stopper. You know that the police can identify people sometimes through prints left by their fingers? That housekeeper, Frenais, knew that I had been to the house before, to seek an appointment. She would tell the police and if they found the stopper they would be certain to accuse me."

"That's the reason you faked the burglary, isn't it?" I said. "You risked staying in the study long enough to open the window and throw some of my uncle's papers around, didn't you? I'll bet you even rumpled his bedclothes so that it looked as if he'd gone to sleep when he usually does. So no one realized anything was wrong until late on the morning after his death. Everyone assumed he was on his way to Le Havre, not lying dead on his study floor behind doors that were normally kept closed."

"If you like to think so, clever girl!"

"I don't *like* anything about it. What if I tell the police all you've just told me?"

Méduse smiled briefly. "You will need to be careful which policeman you choose. Besides, I retrieved my bottle stopper shortly after you and I had our pleasant meeting. There is no other evidence against me besides your word. And in case you are wondering about any lapses of memory from which you seem to have been suffering lately, I have to admit that I hypnotized you into forgetting that you had ever seen me."

"I—I don't believe you!"

"Hypnotism is child's play to me. So are a number of other arcane sciences—transferring thoughts or projecting images over distances, to name two. But this is no time for a lecture. You are going to help me with Dr. Levine?"

"Help *you*?" I exclaimed.

"You gave me your promise," she reminded me.

"That was before you told me how my uncle died."

She frowned. "Then perhaps you'd better give some thought to Dr. Levine's safety."

"Is that a threat?"

"Take it as you wish, my dear."

I forced my voice to sound calm. "I suppose you're planning to hypnotize me into talking him into it?"

Méduse shook her head. "If I were, I should have done so by now and saved all this talk. Unfortunately, one cannot hypnotize people into doing things they are not willing to do."

"Well, I'm not willing to soft-talk Dr. Levine for your benefit, Madame Méduse."

"A pity for you," she answered, glancing significantly beyond me. The man who stood waiting moved slightly and my heart thumped; I'd forgotten just how precarious my position was.

Méduse was watching me intently. She needed only to signal her thug and I would soon be gasping painfully. I couldn't help it—I decided to take the easy way out.

"All right," I said. "I will speak to Dr. Levine. The decision's up to him, anyway."

"Thank you, my dear." Méduse smiled coldly. "Only you *will* persuade him, won't you? You have surely learned by now that if he does not agree, both he and you will suddenly become prone to *accidents*?"

"I told you I'll speak to him," I answered. "I don't make promises I can't keep."

"Splendid! Neither do *I*." She rose. "Now, before you leave, let me show you my little laboratory."

I didn't want to see it. I just wanted to be let go.

"I don't think—" I began, but she shook her head emphatically.

"Just a few more minutes of your time," she insisted. "It is only a simple establishment; yet some of science's greatest achievements have been conceived in modest surroundings."

I saw that she wasn't going to release me until I'd humored her completely. "All right," I said,

and she turned toward another door. The man moved to go with us, and his eyes met mine in a look of pure malice.

Once again I found myself in a room smelling of chemicals with glass and copper apparatus on benches, a Bunsen burner flaring, and liquid steaming and bubbling in a container over it. Two people were at work. One was a stoop-shouldered middle-aged man, peering at his experiment through thick-lensed spectacles. The other was a young girl with hair so blond that it was almost as light as her white lab coat. I thought of a Christmas tree fairy; when she glanced at me, her eyes were cold blue and staring, just like a doll's.

Mme. Méduse snapped an order at them. I was surprised to hear her address them in another language—German, I thought. Without a murmur they quickly left the room. The thug went, too, but stayed waiting at the open door.

Mme. Méduse opened a drawer in a bench. "You really will persuade Dr. Levine?" she asked.

"I told you," I said.

"Promises are easily broken," she said softly. "Perhaps you would keep yours more easily if you were to let me hypnotize you again."

"No!"

I didn't know how much or how little she might be capable of influencing me, but I wasn't going to risk it. I just hoped it was true that she couldn't *force* me to do things.

She accepted my refusal. "Well, then," she

said, "to enable you to assure him from personal experience how harmless my gas is . . ."

She moved swiftly to the door. As she moved I saw her left hand open, and there was the sound of breaking glass. Then a thin vapor drifted up from the floor.

"No—please, no!" I cried. But she had gone through the door and slammed it shut behind her.

The first whiff of vapor reached me, tickling the inside of my nose.

I clapped my hands over my face to cover my nose and mouth.

It was too late. My head began to spin. I staggered. And fell.

CHAPTER
18

A confused noise filled my ears. It was like the baying of wild animals and the shrieking of humans mixed together—a horrible din that was getting louder, coming closer. I realized that I was being chased along a narrow street in the Latin Quarter. I was running as hard as I could, but I couldn't escape the endless maze of winding alleys, and every turn brought me closer to the horrible din.

In a moment I was surrounded by ranks of grim-faced men and women. I had glimpses of pointed caps in stripes of blue, white, and red. Tricolor banners were waved tauntingly in my face.

I wanted to burst through the

cordon, but I knew I wouldn't have the strength. I tried to scream for help or mercy—or just scream—but no sound would come out. I covered my eyes.

Then I felt myself moving. Without actually touching me, the mob was forcing me to go on. A few men and women capered alongside me, making mocking gestures. I thought of trying to run and outdistance them, but I knew it was impossible.

I stumbled on, terrified, and at last ventured a glance back. Many in the crowd carried pitchforks, billhooks, and wooden staves. Others carried poles with straight or curved blades at their ends, bound in red, white, and blue rags. Flame-lit smoke clouds billowed and flickered over their enraged faces, making them appear demonic.

Suddenly the din, which had been rising toward an ear-splitting climax, stopped. Eerie silence reigned. All those tramping feet were suddenly soundless, and there were no more cries, animal or human. It was almost more frightening than the noise had been.

Then I heard the faint sound of a drum. It beat a marching rhythm and the mob fell into step with it. Shoulders and arms swung silently as they marched in procession, and I stumbled along at its head.

I saw that we were approaching a great open space. It was packed with people waving their arms, shaking their fists, shrieking and cackling.

The blue, white, and red emblems were everywhere.

Then I saw two towering posts and a crossbar. Rising slowly to the top of it was a diagonal metallic shape with the shine of steel . . .

The guillotine!

There was a scent—a sickly reek that was familiar to me from back home. It was the stench of stockyards and slaughterhouses.

Blood!

The crowd was enjoying its daily spectacle—and this day I was the leading player in its entertainment. I was being marched to the guillotine.

The women with their knitting sat in the front rows. Gap-toothed gums grinned at me and called out abuse. The platform and the steps loomed nearer. I was taken by the arms and dragged roughly; my legs collapsed and my feet trailed under me as I gave way to the paralysis of fear.

They seemed to be shaking me, trying to force me to walk. A face distorted with rage thrust itself into mine. I shut my eyes to blot out the hideous sight . . .

And I felt a sharp slap on each of my cheeks. My eyes opened.

Méduse's eyes were glittering down at me. "You see, my dear?" she said. "It was nothing. A harmless little sleep of two or three minutes. But a stronger dose would give ample time for an army to overrun its enemy's positions. The French army, the American army! A weapon for our nations that none other could resist!"

Her face was a pale mask of triumph, but all I could see was the guillotine on its platform. The crowd's roar still rang faintly in my ears.

If I closed my eyes again I would be dragged up those steps and thrust across the block. Then the blade would swish down to a last howl from the watchers.

Now I knew how dreadfully Uncle had died and why his expression had been one of such terror. He had been through a horrible nightmare like mine—with one important difference: no one had brought him out of it.

"That is what I refer to as projecting images over distance," Méduse was saying. "Of course, the vapor enhances it. . . ." I barely heard her. Her eyes, so unnaturally bright, held me. It was as if there were an animal alive inside her, an animal that had gone completely mad.

Someone helped me to my feet—evidently all of Méduse's people were there. As I stood up I felt my head clearing fast.

"You'd better sit down again, my dear," Méduse urged me. "Take your time."

I'd spent all the time I was going to in that place. Elbowing her aside, I stumbled toward the door leading to the Métro stairs.

I wrenched it open. There was a blur of white as the blond girl lunged at me. I pushed her aside, and I guess she fell into the others. It gave me time to dash through the door and slam it behind me.

But there wasn't time to think. Common sense

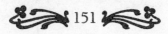

told me to run up the stairs to street level, but instinct won. I took four or five stairs *downward*.

I was out of sight of the door, round the turn of the stairs. I stood absolutely still, pressing my back to the stone wall and holding my breath.

I was only just in time. The door crashed open and I heard agitated voices echoing from above. Then there was the deeper voice of the bodyguard, cursing at the others to get out of his way.

His heavy boots clattered on the stone as he ran out of the hideaway and paused to listen. Méduse shouted "Up! Up!" at him, and the footfalls clattered away up the stairs.

I didn't lose another second, but slipped silently downward, fully expecting some of the others to follow. But I heard no one—only the man's distant cry of anger and frustration.

It was obvious what had happened. He had reached the top and remembered that this unfinished station had its entrance barred and locked. Now he knew—I *couldn't* have escaped that way.

My heart sank. In a moment he would come charging down the stairs. And this time he'd know for sure which way I'd gone.

I'd reached the platform. Now I turned left, caught up my skirts, and ran for my life!

I ran off the end of the platform, onto the track and into the darkness, and I realized that he had me at his mercy. The workmen's train

was still standing where he'd left it. He only had to jump into it and come after me.

There was nothing I could do about my mistake. I could only run on, hoping there wasn't live electricity in the rails and that I wouldn't trip over anything. If I took a fall or sprained an ankle, I'd be helpless.

Anxious as I was to get as far ahead as possible, I slowed to a walk. It was now so dark!

I remembered the headlights that had come on when he'd started the train. "Any moment now," I thought, "they'll come from behind me, and I'll be in their full glare."

But if they lit the way for me, maybe I could run again. The question was, how far to the next station? Could I get there before the train got *me*?

After a few more moments passed, the headlights still had not come on. Surely Méduse hadn't ordered him *not* to chase after me!

The darkness didn't seem quite so bad, now that my eyes were used to it. I even thought I could see a pinprick of light way ahead.

Then I heard footfalls. They were heavy, and they were running. I knew they were his.

But why was he chasing me on foot when he could have used the train? I started to run again.

And soon I saw that there *was* light ahead of me—a growing circle of light where the tunnel led into a station. If only I could reach it and find someone working there who would save me! Surely he couldn't fool them into thinking he was a gendarme again?

The light grew brighter. Sobbing, more for want of breath than from fear, I forced myself on. My pursuer's footfalls grew closer.

Then suddenly the tunnel was bathed in bright light shining from behind me, and I heard a rumbling sound. The train! One of the others must have started it and joined in the chase. How could I hope to beat it? There was no room to get out of its way if it caught up with me.

I forced myself to run even faster. There *were* men working in the station ahead! I tried to call to them, but I could only gasp weakly.

I felt the train behind me like a huge angry iron beast. Then I saw the station ramp and a smocked workman staring into the tunnel.

Like a runner reaching the finish, I threw out my arms and staggered the rest of the way. Behind me there was a sudden bang and a blue flash. He'd shot at me at last—but he'd missed!

There was a loud squeal of brakes, and the train ground to a shuddering halt on the tracks. I no longer cared. "Save me!" I sobbed, and fell into the workman's arms.

CHAPTER
19

Writing this down is one thing. Having it happen was something entirely different.

It was the next morning before life seemed anything like normal again. After a night under yet another of Dr. Levine's sedatives, I awoke in my bed at rue Cambon with warm sunlight streaming through the windows.

Mme. Frenais was standing by the foot of the bed, watching me with motherly concern. "How are you feeling?" she asked before I'd even gotten my eyes fully open.

"I feel fine," I told her. Last night I'd asked about Marcel, but no one had been able to tell me anything. Now I was half-afraid to ask. "Do you know if they found Marcel yet?"

"Someone else must tell you that," she said quickly, and before I could stop her, she left the room.

I was envisioning myself attending Marcel's funeral when the door opened and Marcel walked in. He was even paler than usual, and there was a thick white bandage around his head, but he was smiling and holding a large bouquet of flowers. He came right over and gave me a tight hug and a kiss on each cheek.

"I'm so glad to see you," I said. "It was the worst moment of my life—being dragged away and leaving you lying there."

"If I had been conscious, it would have been *my* worst moment, seeing you go," he replied. "Except that he would have had to kill me before I would have let him take you away."

"I thought he *had* killed you," I said. "He hit you awfully hard."

Marcel shrugged. "It is nothing, only a superficial wound."

There was still something I didn't understand. "Whatever made you go for him like that?"

"Because I knew he was not a policeman. To arrive at just that moment, after Vigny had been telephoning."

"But how could you be so sure?"

"No gendarme in France ever carries a pocket pistol," Marcel answered. "Moreover, every instinct told me he was a fake. And I knew I had to act before he marched us back to Vigny's. I suspect he would have tried to keep me at Vigny's while he pretended to deliver you to the Préfecture."

"You're not far wrong," I said. I looked at Marcel's poor bandaged head. "I suspect that you should never turn your back on an opponent."

He grinned. "I shall remember that in the future."

Dr. Levine, who had been hovering tactfully in the doorway, cleared his throat and came in.

"Did they get her? Méduse?" I asked him.

"Unfortunately, no. Detective Latour and some others went to the Boissière Station and found her apartment—a very clever location for clandestine purposes—but the birds had flown. They had taken almost everything with them— all the chemical apparatus and papers."

"They must have started packing up while he was chasing me," I said.

"No doubt they were prepared for an emergency getaway. Evidently Méduse preferred not to await the outcome of the chase."

"Speaking of the chase, what *did* happen? I remember just reaching safety after he'd fired at me and missed."

The portly doctor shook his head. "He never did fire at you. The bang you heard was the electric current reaching him."

"Electric current? You mean—he was—"

"Those Métro trains activate the live rail up to some forty or fifty feet ahead of themselves. He must have been in contact with the rail when it came alive as the workmen's train approached. They managed to stop the train before it could run over him, but he was dead already."

Although I had no sympathy for the man, I found myself shaking.

"Then if he *had* chased me in the train—"

"Better not think about it," Marcel said. "You came through safely. That's all that matters."

"But who was in the train? Méduse and her people?"

"No," Dr. Levine said. "Workmen. They came on their workshift and boarded it in the usual way, never suspecting that there was anyone on foot in the tunnel. Their driver has been hospitalized with shock."

"Well, I hope they catch that woman soon," I said fervently. "Three murders already, not to mention what might have become of Marcel and me!"

Dr. Levine checked me with an upraised hand. "Softly, softly, my dear. One must be careful not to make accusations which cannot be proved."

"Proved!" I was nearly shouting. "It's obvious! She went to those first two doctors, Brisson and Chautemps, asking for their help. When she told them details of her discovery and they turned her down, she was convinced they would pass off her research as their own. She had them killed in the Métro to stop them."

"Did she admit that?" Marcel asked.

"Well, not in so many words. Oh, can't you

see?" I implored Dr. Levine, who was shaking his head slowly. "All right, I admit Uncle's death *may* have been an accident. But you'd believe me if you'd heard the way she threatened both of us last night."

"I don't disbelieve you, Paris," Dr. Levine said. "But Madame Méduse's work in itself is not criminal and, I repeat, there is no proof of any murders."

"This is ridiculous!" I cried. "Why does everyone want to cover up for that woman? I get arrested and questioned and followed and kidnapped and nearly killed in a tunnel. Marcel gets hit over the head. But everyone else wants to make excuses for poor downtrodden Madame Snakehair! Why, Doctor? Why didn't you want to talk to me about her? And why was Latour so unwilling to listen to my suspicions about Uncle's death?"

Dr. Levine made me feel even crosser by giving Marcel a broad wink and then smiling at me.

"Your answer, my dear Paris, lies in the very way you storm at me. You Americans have a certain reputation among us old-fashioned Europeans. We regard you as headstrong and overconfident, believing that you can settle anything more quickly than we, simply by charging at it head on. *Of course* Monsieur Latour regarded your uncle's death as highly suspicious, especially in conjunction with the other two. *Of course* the woman Méduse was being investigated as a prime suspect. What was lacking was the proof, which you brush aside as unimportant. All of us were afraid that you would feel not enough was being done and would do something rash and imprudent. We wished to prevent that, both for the sake of careful investigation and for your own safety. Now, be fair to us, Paris—was our judgment not absolutely correct? Monsieur Fleury, I ask for your support."

"You have to admit Dr. Levine is right," Marcel told me gravely. "You *did* rather rush into the matter."

"I thought you were my friend!" I said in my best wounded voice. But I was teasing, and they both knew it.

"As a matter of fact," Dr. Levine went on, "I have an appointment at the Préfecture in half an hour to discuss Méduse's case with the commissioner and Latour. I will keep you informed."

After congratulating me yet again on my escape and my quick recovery from the ordeal, the doctor left. Marcel was about to go, too, when I had an inspiration.

"Why don't we go out and have breakfast in a café?" I suggested. "I'm starving. Oh, but your poor head! Perhaps . . ."

"No, no. I'm starving, too. I will wait downstairs."

The café he took me to—on his arm all the way!—was on the rue de Rivoli, looking across the Tuileries Gardens to the river. The proprietress came over with a smile and put a vase of

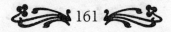

spring flowers on our table. Throughout the delicious breakfast, which *wasn't* just coffee and croissants, she kept giving us secretive smiles, as if she was sure we were sweethearts!

Our conversation wasn't the least bit romantic.

"When you want to catch a wild animal," I said, "you set a trap for it and lie and wait. I read that they catch tigers by tying a young goat to a tree."

"And you regard Madame Méduse as the tiger—*tigress,* I should say? What bait do you propose? Not *yourself*!"

"No, I meant Dr. Levine's consent to help her. That might bring her out of hiding."

Marcel shook his head. "He would not involve himself now. He could not let his name be associated with hers."

"He doesn't have to. But after her threats, she knows that he and I will be expecting trouble. It won't surprise her if he offers his help because he's scared."

"Paris," Marcel said warily, "what have you thought up now?"

"We put an advertisement in the personals column in *Le Matin,* addressed simply to 'Méduse.' She's certain to see it if we let it run a few days, isn't she?"

"I imagine so. Or someone will tell her about it. What will it say?"

"Something like, 'Am prepared to talk regarding collaboration.' No signature. She'll be certain it's from the doctor."

Marcel still looked cautious and puzzled.

"I can't see what comes next. You don't think she would go to his house?"

"Of course not. She'll telephone. He will tell her to meet him somewhere public. We'll be there as well, with the police. When she turns up they'll arrest her. It's simple."

Looking back, I guess it was simple in the other sense, too. I must have been insane to think that a woman of Méduse's intelligence and cunning would walk into a trap as obvious as that.

But believe it or not, she did!

CHAPTER
20

Yes, I know I should at least have *told* Dr. Levine. I ought to have asked his permission. Either way, I know he would have forbidden me to go ahead, and that was the one risk I couldn't take.

Marcel placed the advertisement for me. He wasn't happy about it, but I guess he had started thinking of me as a girl worth humoring. It duly appeared and, of course, everyone saw it—Mme. Frenais, Dr. Levine, and the police.

Dr. Levine was furious. He told me I'd gone too far at last, and he would be cabling my parents immediately. I begged and pleaded, but he was firm. Then I remembered that Uncle's will had not yet

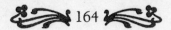

been read, so I pointed out that he had better wait at least until then. He couldn't refuse.

As Uncle's executor he probably knew all the details already, but he wasn't allowed to tell. He just had to swallow his anger and agree not to do anything for the moment.

Latour blustered about having me arrested for hindering police inquiries. I argued that I had done nothing of the sort. I suggested that if Mme. Méduse did take the bait, the police would need to have a plan ready. He scoffed at that, but I heard him, on the quiet, tell Dr. Levine that if he did get a message from Méduse he should suggest a meeting in the Great Gallery of the Louvre Museum. When I passed that on to Marcel, he told me that it is where the *Mona Lisa* hangs.

Méduse didn't telephone Dr. Levine—she telephoned *me*! She demanded to know what was behind the doctor's advertisement: was it a police trap? Although the menace in her tone sent chills right through me, I was able to answer truthfully that it had been inserted without the police knowing.

"I promised I would persuade Dr. Levine at least to talk to you," I said. "I told you I keep my promises."

There was a moment's silence, then a husky chuckle. "You're a remarkable girl, *Liebchen*," she said. "You and I could be great allies and friends."

"Humph!" I wanted to say; but I bit my tongue

and told her the proposed meeting place. She named a time the next day.

Dr. Levine was flabbergasted by my news when I telephoned him. A little later M. Latour called me, demanding to know if I was speaking the truth. I simply said that he must take it or leave it. I sounded braver than I felt.

If Méduse didn't show up after all, Latour would be furious, and that was not a pleasant prospect. Also, I couldn't help feeling a little bad about Méduse herself. Although I was convinced she was dangerous and quite possibly insane, I didn't like betraying her. Despite all she'd done, she held a kind of fascination for me. Perhaps it was the animal quality I saw in her. Even though it may be necessary, there is something criminal in caging a tiger.

"Don't be hard on yourself," Marcel urged me. "Think of that roughneck of hers. It shouldn't be difficult—you still have the bruises he inflicted on you. And think of your uncle."

"I know. But when someone puts their trust in you and you break it, what does that make you?"

So my feelings were thoroughly mixed the next morning as Marcel and I made our way to the Louvre. We walked through gallery after gallery of classical statues, Egyptian mummies, bronzes, vases, and other ancient treasures before we even reached the picture galleries. As we walked, I took careful note of every woman we passed. Méduse would surely be disguised, I thought, although if she wore her armlet as a kind of charm, she would probably be too superstitious to leave it off. I began looking at arms and sleeves as well as faces.

At last we reached the Great Gallery on the second floor. There, with a crowd around her, was No. 1601, Leonardo da Vinci's *La Gioconda*, better known as *Mona Lisa*.

"What do you think?" Marcel asked when we got our turn to look at her up close.

"She's smaller than I expected. And the paint's darker. I'm not sure I'd call that the best picture in the world."

"The best known, though," he assured me.

We made way for the other spectators. If she was coming at all, Mme. Méduse would soon be among them.

"There's Dr. Levine," Marcel said. The doctor, in frock coat, spats, gloves, and top hat, was viewing pictures on a side wall. "We'd better stay away from him, though I'm sure she expects you to be here, and she knows you have a young man friend."

I couldn't resist giving his arm a squeeze for that. He pressed mine, too, and smiled briefly at me.

"I don't see any police," I remarked.

"Latour is the only one you would recognize, isn't he?"

"Méduse knows him too," I said. "He would hardly show himself."

We wandered on, trying not to be too obvious

about looking at people instead of artworks. Not for the first time, I wondered how Holmes always managed to be so observant without calling attention to himself—I would have loved to stand there with a set of binoculars! I settled for taking another casual glance around the gallery. No Méduse. I began to believe she wasn't going to appear, and the thought was almost a relief.

Marcel suddenly said, "Look! Someone's speaking to Dr. Levine. Is it Méduse?"

She was slim, tall, and erect, fashionably outfitted in a pink wool suit and a large hat adorned with silk roses and a patterned white veil. Her hair was auburn, though.

"A wig?" Marcel suggested when I mentioned it.

"Let's get nearer."

We edged around the gallery until we were close enough to see Dr. Levine's face. He didn't look as if he was merely chatting with someone he happened to know. He was listening attentively while the woman talked. She was rather like Mme. Méduse, and yet . . .

Things happened quickly then. They began innocuously when Dr. Levine took off his hat and turned it slowly in his hands. Then two frock-coated gentlemen detached themselves from the throng and began moving toward one of the doorways, keeping their eyes on Dr. Levine and the woman as they went.

"Police," said Marcel. "The hat was a signal."

A more dramatic development was caused by

another man who was sitting across the gallery with the copyists. I'd noticed him earlier. He was quite handsome and had a rather aristocratic bearing—instead of hunching forward like most of the other copyists, he sat up straight on his stool with his head tilted back almost haughtily and his little pointed black beard jutting forward toward his canvas. He wore a floppy black hat with a broad brim and a paint-stained smock, and I wondered if he was someone famous before I realized that famous artists weren't likely to sit copying in galleries, not even in the Louvre.

Suddenly, though, he was far from dignified: he jumped to his feet and began raving at his canvas as though it had offended him. Then he hurled his palette to the floor. He reversed his long brush, and using the point of its stem, he slashed violently at the work he'd been doing.

A uniformed attendant ran toward him and the artist gave his easel a violent push. It went crashing into the attendant and sent him sprawling. Still raving and cursing, the artist pushed people aside and hurtled out through the nearest doorway, his long legs flying and his smock streaming behind.

Everyone's attention had been riveted by this extraordinary exhibition—with one exception. As I glanced back toward Dr. Levine I was just in time to glimpse a disappearing flash of pink skirt. The woman who had been talking with the doctor dashed out through another exit.

The detectives had been as distracted as everyone else by the disturbance and were looking around blankly. Dr. Levine clapped his hands furiously for their attention and pointed to the way the woman had gone. The policemen ran after her.

"Shall we?" Marcel asked eagerly, prepared to join the chase. I didn't move.

"They won't catch her," I said. "Anyway, she's the wrong one."

Dr. Levine had joined us fulminating about the "incompetent cretins" of policemen who had obeyed his signal and then let themselves be distracted like that.

"But it wasn't Madame Méduse speaking to you, was it, Doctor?" I asked.

"Ah, you realized that? No, she was an emissary from Méduse. She had instructions to take me to her, if I agreed to cooperate. I said I would and then gave the arranged signal to warn those fools to follow us."

"Where were you going?"

"She would not say. But it was not far."

"Just to the other end of the gallery," I told him.

"Eh? What's that?"

"Where Méduse was sitting at her easel. She was the one who caused that commotion. She had the perfect vantage point to spot a trap. When she saw it, she was ready with a diversion that gave both of them a chance to get away."

Dr. Levine replaced his hat. "Paris," he said, "I think I shall have to talk seriously with Latour about having you join the force. *If* you are staying on in our country, that is."

"It's my country, too, in a way," I said in reply. When I looked at Marcel, he was smiling broadly at me.

A few days later a small package arrived at the house in rue Cambon, addressed to me. I unwrapped it and found a wooden box and a note inside. I opened the note first.

"Mona Lisa is not the only woman with secrets, *Liebchen*," I read. "I was a little too smart for you this time, but you made a brave opponent and I salute you. As a reward, I think you should have something that was intended for you in the first place. My late bodyguard must have stolen it from your uncle's study on that night when he caught you outside and interrupted my search. It has been found among his belongings, for which he has no further use."

It was signed, "Until we meet again—Méduse."

There was a P.S.: "Whether you care to believe it or not, it *was* an accident."

So this was the mysterious wooden box that was stolen in the burglary-that-never-was! I opened it gingerly, half afraid of what I would find.

It was lined with black velvet and contained a gold ring set with two beautiful sapphires. There was an inscription in tiny lettering on the inside of the band: *"Pour ma chère Paris, bienvenue!"*

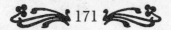

Poor Uncle. I thanked him silently for his kind, loving thought. My welcome to Paris had been very different from the one he'd intended, but in spite of that I did feel welcome now.

I slipped the ring on my finger. The blue sapphires winked at me and made me think of other jewel-eyes, those ruby eyes of flashing red. Would I ever see them—and that remarkable creature, half-serpent, half-tigress—again?

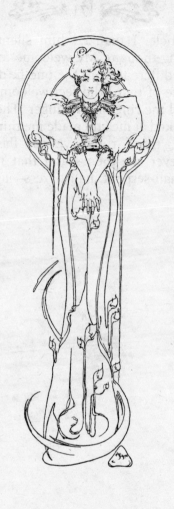